DAWN KNOX

FEARLESS HEART

Complete and Unabridged

LINFORD
Leicester

First published in Great Britain in 2019

First Linford Edition
published 2021

A catalogue record for this book is available
from the British Library.

ISBN 978–1–4448–4624–9

Published by
Ulverscroft Limited
Anstey, Leicestershire

Set by Words & Graphics Ltd.
Anstey, Leicestershire
Printed and bound in Great Britain by
TJ Books Ltd., Padstow, Cornwall

This book is printed on acid-free paper

1

1940

The German pilot released his last bomb over RAF Holsmere, then banking sharply, set off for home. Beneath him, the anti-aircraft crew aimed and fired, scoring a direct hit. As the pilot bailed out of the aircraft and his parachute hung momentarily in the night sky, the flaming wreckage spiralled to earth, crashing somewhere near Chelmsford.

His bomb fell close to the operations block and the explosion rocked the ops room causing the lights to flicker and plaster to rain down from the ceiling onto the girls below. Several people coughed, clearing dust from their throats, but no one panicked and no one left their post despite the air raid warning having sounded shortly before the German aerial attack began.

Lumps of plaster bounced off the WAAFs' tin helmets, landing on the plotting table around which they stood as they pushed counters across the map with their rods.

Genevieve swept debris off the table with one hand, while with the other, she deftly moved a counter with her pole. Above her, on a raised gallery, RAF officers avidly watched the counters which showed the progress of the aircraft currently over their sector of the British Isles, all the while, painstakingly relaying that information into their telephone mouthpieces.

Genevieve clenched her teeth as another explosion — closer than the last — shook the ops room dislodging a large piece of plaster that hit the map with a puff of dust and shattered into smaller fragments. The WAAF next to her brushed the pieces away then advanced her counter.

The deep booms of the explosions and the *ack-ack* of the anti-aircraft guns outside on the airfield were so loud, Genevieve struggled to hear the messages coming through her set. With her brows drawn together, she pressed the headphones tightly to her ears and tried to filter out everything except the information being transmitted to her from a local radar station.

In June, after France fell to the German army, the new prime minister, Winston Churchill, declared the Battle of France was over and the Battle of Britain was about to begin. Hitler's planned invasion of Britain had started with the Luftwaffe trying to take control of the skies over southern England, firstly by attacking coastal targets and British shipping, then by moving inland and destroying communications centres and airfields — one of which, was RAF Holsmere situated in the Essex countryside.

The WAAFs in the ops room were becoming used to the regular aerial bombardment since the station had been targeted repeatedly, along with

3

others in their sector, but Hitler had underestimated the skill of the RAF pilots who defended the skies over Britain, as well as the determination of the ground crews keeping airfields operational. Everyone was doing their bit to prevent the Luftwaffe conquering the skies.

Genevieve checked the clock on the wall. Another five minutes had passed in the blink of an eye. The station's Vickers Wellington Bombers were due back and she knew any damage outside was being repaired to make the runways safe for the squadron's aircraft. One of them would not be coming back. Genevieve knew that already because the crew had sent a mayday call, after which there'd been silence. One of the other pilots reported seeing the aircraft plunge into the Channel after it had been shelled.

The lost bomber had been H for Harry. Genevieve knew the crew well but there was no time for grief. She and the other girls had a job to do and they'd remain at the plotting table until they were relieved at the end of their shift. By that time, the Wellingtons and their crews should be safely home. Hopefully.

She sent up a silent prayer for Sonny, pilot of P for Pip. He wasn't her sweetheart, although if he'd given her any sign that he wanted her to be more than a friend, she'd have been very willing. She knew it would never be. Sonny had been stepping out with her friend Ellie. They seemed to be made for each other but inexplicably he'd broken it off. Since then, he'd taken Genevieve out twice but she could tell his heart wasn't in it. Perhaps he regretted finishing with Ellie. Or perhaps his work as a pilot required all his attention. Whatever the reason, she knew that Sonny, with the beautiful, dark eyes, would never be hers. It was probably just as well because it was her last week at RAF Holsmere and this was her final shift. On Monday, she'd begin a new role in London.

Genevieve listened to her roommate's rhythmic breathing coming from the other bed. Jess had been asleep when she'd returned to their billet, Larkrise Farm, but Genevieve knew Jess would soon be up to start an early shift. They were both plotters, though on different shifts, and they were both leaving RAF Holsmere to start new work.

Quiet, straight-laced Jess would soon be going to Bletchley Park, a place Genevieve had never heard of. Inexplicably, Jess had decided to become a clerk. Why Jess wanted to exchange work as a plotter to go and shuffle paper, Genevieve couldn't imagine. But Jess was a quiet girl whose idea of a good evening was to curl up with a mug of cocoa and a book of crossword puzzles.

Genevieve, on the other hand, loved to be outside. She often went for long walks in the woods around the farm and on several occasions, had swum in the river. The water had been freezing but exhilarating. She'd only decided against going again because Jess told her that several of the pilots had gone swimming near her usual spot and when they'd come out, discovered their clothes had been taken as a joke by members of their crew. It was typical of the pranks the airmen played on each other and the story of the three officers returning to base with leafy boughs to hide their modesty had been told with great relish in the Wild Boar pub for the next few nights.

Robert Barnes, one of those naked pilot officers who'd put up with all the ribbing, had been one of the men who hadn't returned from the mission over Germany earlier. Genevieve couldn't believe he'd gone. He'd been twenty-years old. The same age as her. She shook her head trying to banish the thought of a young life wasted.

It wasn't like the Germans weren't losing men either. Last night, she knew five of their Junkers Ju 88s had been shot out of the sky. For them, the war was over — either dead or imprisoned, they wouldn't fight again. This conflict was a tragedy of unbelievable proportions.

Genevieve turned over and pulled the blankets higher but it was hard to calm her mind and sleep after such a dramatic night. At least Sonny and his crew had returned safely in P for Pip. And Sonny's friend Leo and his crew had returned too.

In the bedroom across the landing, Ellie and Kitty were presumably sleeping now. They were WAAFs too and the four girls had arrived on the same day at RAF Holsmere and were billeted together in Larkrise Farm. For a while, it looked as though Ellie and Sonny would become sweethearts. Even more briefly, it appeared that Kitty and Leo would as well. But where Ellie and Sonny's brief relationship had been like two candles glowing brightly together before a puff of wind had extinguished them both, Kitty and Leo's relationship flickered repeatedly as they seemed incapable of committing to each other for more than a day or so. Leo's roving eye would fall on another girl and Kitty would waste no time flirting with another man. Such waste!

Everywhere Genevieve looked, there was waste. Countless lives being squandered each day and even when people had time and opportunity, they couldn't see the precious gifts they'd been given.

Her mother had been most insistent that she and her brother use all the gifts they were lucky enough to possess. That was one reason why Genevieve was leaving RAF Holsmere. Being bilingual was definitely a gift and one she was sure would help her make a better contribution to the war effort than as a plotter. Not that her current job wasn't worthwhile, but she'd mastered it quickly and was sure others would too, so she would be easily replaced. However, a lifetime of living in both France and England had ensured she was fluent in both languages, speaking without a foreign accent in either, and familiar with the idioms and expressions in both countries. Her language skills would be vital in her new job.

Finally, exhaustion claimed her and she drifted off to sleep, waking late when the sun was streaming through the window. Considerate Jess had risen silently and crept out so as not to wake her, then left for the base.

When Genevieve went downstairs for breakfast, Kitty was holding a mug of tea in both hands staring wistfully into space.

'That was a lively night last night,' she said, 'Was there much damage on the base?'

'Mostly the runway and one of the hangars,' Genevieve said, then guessing what was really on Kitty's mind added, 'Leo got back safely.'

'And the others?' Kitty asked casually although Genevieve wasn't fooled.

'Everyone except H for Harry's crew.'

Kitty shook her head and sighed, 'How awful. But thank you for letting me know about Leo.'

'Are you two back together?' Genevieve asked.

'He only has eyes for Connie Stamford now.'

'I'm sorry, Kitty.'

'Oh, don't be sorry for me, I've got a date with a new pilot. He's only just arrived at Holsmere and he's ever so handsome and dashing.'

'Kitty!' Genevieve said in reproach.

'But don't you worry, darling, it won't spoil our evening tonight.'

'Oh . . . about that . . . ' Genevieve said, wanting to emphasise once again she didn't want to do anything too outrageous, if only for Jess's sake.

Kitty held up her hand, 'It's all arranged. Don't worry. You and Jess'll love it. I'd better go. I've to drive Group Captain Jennings to Hornchurch.'

Genevieve groaned inwardly, an evening arranged by Kitty would involve lots of alcohol and men, neither of which would please Jess who didn't approve of Kitty's lifestyle. How gentle

Ellie put up with her roommate's excesses, Genevieve couldn't guess, although Ellie had once let slip she thought Kitty's behaviour was an attempt to find acceptance and love. Despite Kitty's gaiety, there was a hint of sadness about her as if her brashness and confidence were merely a mask. Whatever the reason for Kitty's behaviour, she and Jess would have to put up with whatever she'd laid on. Hopefully, if it was too shocking, Ellie would be able to restrain her. If not . . . well, it was only one night, and their last together.

It was strange to think she'd completed her last day at work here. Her body had become accustomed to the rhythm of the shifts and she loved the camaraderie. Now her departure was imminent, sadness washed over her. Later she would go to see her senior WAAF officer to be dismissed and do the rounds saying goodbye to everyone. It wouldn't take long to pack her kitbag and Jess, who liked to be organised had already done hers, ready for the morning when they'd be off together to the station.

After breakfast, Genevieve went back to her room. She took her few belongings out of her drawer and placed them on the bed ... the fountain pen her father had given her, notepaper and envelopes, a framed photograph of her family standing in her grandfather's vineyard in the Loire Valley, some French perfume and a small box. Genevieve raised the lid of the box and sighed as she took the small silver heart charm out and balanced it on the end of her forefinger.

Such a bitter-sweet gift. Poor Sonny! He'd planned to explain before he gave it to her on her birthday that it was to bring her luck. His mother had given him a heart-shaped locket with photographs of his family and he wore it all the time. So in his mind hearts represented good luck. It was only after he'd bought it that he realised how it might be misconstrued and Genevieve might get the wrong idea and think it a declaration of love. He'd been mortified when Leo had snatched it from him and given it to her before he could explain. As soon as she'd raised the a quick glance at Sonny's face told her all she needed to know. Before anyone saw the contents, she'd replaced the lid and slipped the box in her pocket.

Later, she told Sonny she couldn't accept the gift but he'd explained he intended it to be a good luck charm and asked her to keep it, so she did.

If only he *had* given it to her as a love token!

Yet she knew that would never happen and seeing him all the time was becoming torment. She wondered if she ought to tell him she'd changed her mind and was unable to accept it but she knew he'd be embarrassed if she reminded him of the gift which she was sure he'd forgotten about. No, she'd keep it. It might bring her luck, even if it hadn't brought her any regarding Sonny.

'I'm dreading this evening,' Jess said as she pinned her hair up, 'Can't you tell Kitty and Ellie I'm not well?'

'They know you're fine, Jess,' Genevieve said, 'Come on, it's our last evening together, please try and enjoy yourself.'

The two girls went downstairs. The owners of Larkrise Farm, Mr and Mrs Ringwood allowed the girls to use the kitchen during the day when they were out on the farm but preferred them to go to their rooms in the evening.

Kitty and Ellie were waiting for them at the long wooden table, on which was a wind-up gramophone and a pile of records.

'It's all right,' Kitty said when she saw their startled faces, 'Mrs Ringwood's gone to her sister's and Mr Ringwood's in the Wild Boar and won't be back until late, so we can make as much noise as we like. Now, would you like tea or cocoa?'

Genevieve asked, 'Aren't we going out?'

'No, I thought you might like to stay home on your last night,' Kitty said, looking crestfallen, 'Oh, no! I'm sorry, would you rather have gone to the Wild Boar?'

'No,' said Jess quickly, 'This is wonderful!'

'Oh, good!' said Kitty, 'I so wanted you to enjoy this evening.'

'We have cakes, and Kitty's managed to get a box of chocolates,' Ellie said, sorting through the pile of records, 'How about Fred Astaire's *Cheek to Cheek*? I love that song.'

By the time Mr Ringwood, relieved of his wife's critical eye for one evening, staggered home, the girls were dancing with each other to the music from the gramophone. Despite the lack of men and alcohol, even Kitty was having a good time.

'My stomach muscles ache,' Jess said later when they broke up the party to go to their room, 'I don't think I've laughed so much in my life!'

'That was a very thoughtful send-off Kitty and Ellie gave us,' Genevieve said as she got into bed. 'It wasn't the sort of evening Kitty would normally like but even she seemed to have fun.'

'She *was* the fun,' Jess said. 'That impersonation she did of Flight Officer Bentley! I've never seen anything so hilarious. Kitty should be on the stage, she's wasted here . . . but now I feel very mean for all the horrid thoughts I've said about her in the past.'

'Poor Kitty. It's like she's lost her way.'

Jess paused for a moment and then said, 'You know, Genevieve, you always look deeper than I do. I don't suppose I'd have spotted that myself but you're right. I feel very ashamed of myself for not having seen past that brazen façade. That's one thing I'll always remember about you . . . your kindness and your tolerance.'

⋆ ⋆ ⋆

Despite the late night, the girls were up early to share a last breakfast together and to ensure the kitchen was spotless for Mrs Ringwood's return.

The hilarity of the previous evening had been replaced by wistfulness and sadness.

'You will both write, won't you?' said Ellie.

'Oh, yes,' said Jess, 'And I want to know everything that's going on here at Holsmere.'

'You'll soon forget all about us when you've got new friends,' said Ellie.

Genevieve was grateful no one had pressed her about writing. Her dream was to go back to France, behind enemy lines, and there would be no letters from her while she was there.

Her parents were both working with Charles de Gaulle, who'd arrived in England several months before, and after his BBC broadcast in June when he'd invited members of the French armed forces who'd fled France to join him and continue the fight, he'd become known as the leader of the Free French. 'France is not alone!' he said, urging his countrymen to join him, 'Whatever happens, the flame of French resistance must not and shall not die.'

Genevieve loved both countries equally and had taken de Gaulle's appeal literally. If humanly possible, she intended to return to France and do what she could to resist the German occupation.

'Come on, dreamy!' Jess said and Genevieve realised she'd been so lost in her thoughts, the others were ready and waiting for her.

The four girls walked to the base for the last time, Ellie and Kitty to go on duty and Jess and Genevieve to catch the lorry which was going to the railway station in town. Several other WAAFs and airmen stopped to say goodbye when they saw the girls hugging each other tearfully, until the sergeant driving the truck bellowed that if they didn't get aboard he'd leave without them.

Grabbing the rope and hoisting themselves over the tailboard, Jess and Genevieve sat on the uncomfortable bench, clutching their kitbags. As the truck accelerated away from the base the girls were silent, looking back at the place they'd called home for what seemed like a life time.

'I didn't think I'd be upset to leave,' Jess said.

'You're not regretting your decision, are you?'

'No,' Jess said hesitantly, then added more firmly, 'No, not at all. Even though it was a bit unexpected.'

'Unexpected? You don't seem to be the sort of person who does things unexpectedly.'

'It was that crossword puzzle competition. I sent off my entry and a few days later, I received an invitation to go to London for an interview.'

'When did that happen?'

'Just before my last leave. In the letter, I was told not to say. So I told you I was going to stay with my parents for a few days, but I stopped off in London. I'm not really allowed to say what happened but it's the reason I'm going to Bletchley Park.'

'Oh, you dark horse!' Genevieve said — because she too had attended an interview and not told the others.

At Liverpool Street Station they got off the train and stood looking at each other, neither wanting to be the first to say goodbye and signal the end of their friendship. They hadn't been close like Ellie and Kitty but they'd come to respect each other. They both knew their new roles would be all-consuming and that promises to keep in touch might not be kept. Finally, with a sigh, Genevieve stepped forward and hugged Jess. They clung to each other for several minutes, hiding their tears.

* * *

As soon as Jess was swallowed up by the crowd and Genevieve could no longer see her, the sadness lifted. There was now nothing to remind her of her life at Holsmere and the gloom that had descended on her when she'd woken this morning was replaced by anticipation and excitement. Jess's new job obviously involved secret war work and Genevieve couldn't begin to imagine what it could be, but it wouldn't be as dangerous as what she planned to do. Jess hated walking to the base in the dark on her own, so the thought of working in Occupied France would terrify her!

Genevieve had always been daring and when she was young, she'd competed with her elder brother, Jean-Paul, or JP as she called him. He'd always been fearless to the point of reckless and between them they'd given their mother many worrying moments. She was looking forward to seeing her brother and parents, even if it was only for one evening. Knowing she was coming home, everyone had managed to get one night's leave before they all returned the following day and Genevieve started her new job.

Turning off the High Road, Genevieve felt a rush of pleasure as she walked along the street where she'd been brought up while in England. Her parents' other home was in the Loire Valley, in her grandfather's estate at Château Saint Pierre. It had been those vineyards which had brought Genevieve's parents together years before. Her grandfather, Hugh Lawrence travelled regularly to the Loire Valley to sample the wines made in the area and to place orders for those he liked.

When his son Dennis was seventeen, Hugh took him on one of his wine-tasting trips, eager to train him to take over the buying. Although he always found pleasure in tasting the wines and visiting the French wine-growing regions, increasingly, Hugh dreaded the travel, especially the boat trip across the Channel. Once Dennis was familiar with what was required, Hugh intended to send him to France on his own to select and purchase the wines for the family business. Lawrence Wine Merchants was a well-established company based in Mayfair, London, which had been in the family since the 1700's and Hugh had every confidence in his son's ability to carry on the business.

Dennis was outgoing and sociable as well as knowledgeable about wines and he soon became well-known among the vineyard owners. But it was the Château Saint Pierre near Saumur in the Loire Valley which always received his full attention.

The area's limestone soil grew grapes that were perfect for sparkling wine production and Dennis bought cases of wine from many of the vineyards in the region. But there was an added attraction at the Château Saint Pierre — the vineyard owner's daughter, Lucienne Vannier.

Dennis fell in love with the sixteen-year-old girl the moment he set eyes on her but her father was very protective and although Lucienne made it clear she liked the young Englishman, she knew her father would not be happy about such a match. Not that he disliked Dennis — far from it — but he was an autocratic man who was slow to change his mind once it was made up.

When Lucienne was eighteen, she ran away from home and travelled to England with Dennis who married her immediately and set up home in Greenwich, in the same house towards which Genevieve was now heading.

The front door opened and her mother ran down the path towards the gate.

'Ma chérie! Oh, how wonderful to see you!' She held Genevieve tightly, only releasing her when her husband appeared and demanded to give his daughter a hug.

'You're thinner, Pipsqueak,' JP said, calling her by his pet nickname and playfully pushing her.

'And you're much fatter, Miney,' she said, shoving him back.

'Good gracious, why can't you two

ever be nice to each other?' Lucienne asked with a proud smile at her two children.

* * *

The conversation over dinner was lively as the Lawrence family reminisced about the time they'd spent in France. They discussed the past and spoke about the distant future when they'd return. No one mentioned the current occupation of their beloved country. To have done so, would have breathed life into the unbelievable, and remind them they were not at liberty to visit Lucienne's father, Bernard Vannier, nor her brother Alexandre who were both still in France.

As a young man, Alexandre had been keen to involve himself in the running of the château but his father refused to implement any of his suggestions or to listen to his son's ideas. Eventually, there'd been an enormous row and Alexandre had given an ultimatum

— either his father listened and at least considered his opinions, or he would leave and not return.

Alexandre had left and never returned.

Bernard's wife died when Lucienne was twelve and he'd never remarried, so he lived alone in Château Saint Pierre. After a long period of silence and several apologetic letters from Lucienne, Bernard finally decided to forgive her for running off to England and marrying Dennis without his permission. The dispute had soon been forgotten when, two months after the reconciliation, his first grandchild, Jean-Paul was born. Bernard adored JP and doted on Genevieve when she came along two years later and was never happier than when his family were around him at the château. From time to time, Lucienne tried to persuade her father to contact her brother, Alexandre, but Bernard always refused.

'If Alexandre wanted to see me, he would come,' he'd say.

'Papa, it takes two to make an argument. Why not write and see how he is?'

After Alexandre had left the château, he'd moved to a small village in Normandy where he'd worked on a farm and learned how to make cider and the region's famous apple brandy, Calvados. He married the farmer's daughter and when her parents died, she and Alexandre had inherited the farm. Bernard only knew this because Lucienne had told him and nagged him incessantly to contact his son, but his pride was too great.

Once the Germans had occupied France, Lucienne rarely heard from her father and brother, receiving letters they posted to her cousin in Spain which he forwarded to England. To her great sadness, neither Bernard nor Alexandre mentioned they were in contact with the other.

'So, Pipsqueak, you start your new post tomorrow?' JP said now.

Genevieve nodded. So far, no one

had mentioned work. Her parents assisted the Free French and she knew her brother worked for the Special Operations Executive, a newly-formed and secret British organisation set up to carry out clandestine work to help win the war. And tomorrow, she would join them too.

'You're not worried about it are you?' he asked.

'No, I'm looking forward to it.'

'Good. The SOE are doing some really important work in France,' he said, avoiding mentioning any part he might play in that work.

Lucienne looked at her daughter, a younger version of her, and her son who was a younger version of her husband and smiled with pride.

'Let's have a toast!' she said, topping up everyone's glass with wine from her father's vineyard, 'To us all. And to the next time we're all together enjoying a bottle of wine on Château Saint Pierre land.'

They clinked glasses.

'I came across your poems the other day, Maman,' JP said, 'Have you written any lately?'

Lucienne laughed, 'No, I haven't the time. But I was never very good at it anyway.'

'Nonsense!' said Dennis, 'You wrote me some beautiful love poems.'

'Dennis! Don't embarrass me!' Lucienne said, cheeks reddening, 'Not in front of the children.'

'I think they're old enough not to be shocked now, darling!'

'Which poem was it, JP?' Genevieve asked.

'The one about the rainbow.'

Genevieve tilted her head to one side and thought back to when her mother had first written the poem several years ago.

'Now, how did it begin? Ah yes . . . A rainbow is a promise that's painted in the sky, Assurance that the greyest clouds are merely passing by.'

Her brother chimed in with the rest, 'However long the storm may last,

30

however dark the sky. The sun will once again return, on that you can rely.'

'Fancy you both remembering that!' Lucienne said with pride.

'And what an appropriate verse for our times,' Dennis said, 'Let's drink a toast to peace — and the sun returning again.'

'To peace.'

Each person smiled and raised their glass, determination and resolve burning in their eyes.

★   ★   ★

Genevieve was disappointed to find JP had already left when she got up the following morning.

'You know how he hates goodbyes,' Lucienne said as she handed her daughter a slice of toast, 'And he had a very early start. He's off somewhere and I don't think we'll see him again for some time.' Lucienne lowered her gaze and swallowed hard, as if fighting back

31

tears. 'And now you're off to join SOE too.' She brushed a piece of fluff off her daughter's jacket and straightened her tie. 'Please take care, chérie . . . '

'Of course I will, Maman.'

Genevieve arrived in London early and found Orchard Court, a white mansion block, on the east side of Portman Square. The doorman, in dark suit and tie, led her into the building to the gilded gates of the lift and escorted her to a flat on the second floor.

'We use this as a waiting room,' he explained leading her into the bathroom, 'and since you're rather early . . . '

Genevieve looked about in amazement. Surely this was a joke? But not long after, the doorman reappeared and asking her to follow him, he led her along a corridor to an office.

'Major Buckmaster,' he said as he ushered her into the room.

Genevieve saluted and then shook the major's hand before he offered her a chair.

Major Maurice Buckmaster, the head

of F Section which was concerned with operations in France, perched on the edge of his desk and welcomed her warmly. He was obviously familiar with her background as he switched to speaking in French and chatted about her last post at RAF Holsmere.

'You'll be required to sign the Official Secrets Act before you're briefed any further,' he said and slid some papers in front of her. 'Do you have any objections to that?'

'No, sir.' Genevieve signed the papers.

'You cannot discuss your work with anyone outside SOE. Do you understand, Miss Lawrence?'

'Yes, sir.'

'Very good. Well, now the formalities are complete, I'll take you along to Miss Atkins, the Intelligence Officer for F Section. What Miss Atkins doesn't know about our work isn't worth knowing. She'll give you the papers you need, a travel warrant and details of your job. You'll be working in a country house in Kent. Any questions?'

Genevieve hesitated. 'Well, sir, I rather thought I'd be going to France.'

'France?' Major Buckmaster looked startled, 'Oh no! I'm afraid that won't be possible at all.'

'But I thought in France, I would — '

'Definitely not. All our agents are male. It's not our policy I'm afraid.'

'I thought with my knowledge of the country and the language I could be of use . . . '

'Even so, I'm afraid that simply won't be possible. But don't worry, your linguistic skills will be put to good use and you'll be doing vital work for the war effort.'

'Yes, sir.' Genevieve was bitterly disappointed.

'Now, if you'll follow me to Miss Atkins' office, she'll be able to tell you more about the job.'

He led her further down the hall to another office and once he'd introduced her to the severe woman seated at the desk, he shook Genevieve's hand

and wished her luck.

Miss Atkins was tall, slim and smartly-dressed in a tweed suit, her fair hair rolled up at the nape of her neck. She rose, greeted Genevieve and asked her to sit.

Major Buckmaster hadn't exaggerated when he praised the Intelligence Officer's knowledge of the running of the department — and of the newest recruit. She knew a great deal about Genevieve and her family, mentioning that JP was a trusted member of the department, and that she knew about her parents' links with Charles de Gaulle's Free French.

'I understand you ski and have some experience of mountain climbing,' Miss Atkins said.

How did this woman know so much about her?

'Now, the job you will be required to do . . . ' Miss Atkins said, finally telling Genevieve about her new role.

'Each of the wireless operators we've placed in France has a person in

England dedicated to listening for their messages. We call these people 'godfathers', or indeed, 'godmothers'. You will be a godmother. Each operator in France has a specific time when they are due to come on air and send a message, this is known as their schedule, more commonly shortened to 'sched'. You will come on duty half an hour before your agent's sched and listen in to their wavelength. When they are on air, you will take down their message and reply. Full training will be given.'

Miss Atkins gave Genevieve all her documents, and details on how to get to the house near Sevenoaks where she would be living and working.

'Any questions?' Miss Atkins asked.

'No, madam,' Genevieve said wanting to enquire about the possibility of going to France but not daring to ask. Major Buckmaster had made it clear it wouldn't be possible.

★ ★ ★

On arriving at the large country house, Genevieve was met by a tall, blonde girl, who was a sergeant in the First Aid Nursing Yeomanry, or FANY. Judging by the number of khaki uniforms Genevieve had seen since she'd arrived, there were many FANY girls working in the radio listening and transmission station.

'This is the room you'll be sharing with Diana Beckford,' the sergeant said. 'She's been here a few months, so she'll show you the ropes. Now, if you'd like to leave your kit bag here, I'll show you the mess and other places you need to know, then I'll take you to see the commanding officer.'

Genevieve spent the next few weeks training to send and receive wireless messages, working closely with the operator she'd be taking over from. Eileen had recently married and once she knew she was pregnant, she'd decided she wanted to do war work which had more predictable hours.

It had been her job to be on duty

whenever 'her' agent in France — code name Jaguar — was due to come on air. She arrived half an hour before his sched was due to begin, and then remained at her station until her agent had finished. Usually, it was quite predictable because an agent's scheds were at fixed times but if he was on the run, he might not be able to keep to the scheds and may, indeed, not be able to use his wireless at all.

At those times, Eileen would work around the clock with another operator, so that whenever the agent came on air, his message would be received. She admitted to Genevieve she was finding it a bit much because Jaguar had gone missing for a week before he'd managed to locate a safe house and been able to keep to regular sched times again.

Eileen showed Genevieve how to recognise Jaguar's 'fist'. This was the technique he used when sending Morse Code messages which was unique and as distinctive as a person's handwriting.

'It's to do with the pressure each

agent uses when tapping out the code on the key of their transmitter and the length of time between taps,' Eileen said. 'If their fist changes dramatically, you have to alert a senior officer because it's likely their wireless has fallen into enemy hands and someone is posing as your agent. But don't panic if his fist is only slightly different from usual because it may be he's sending messages on the run and if he's in a hurry, he may not be as careful as normal. The Germans have Radio Direction Finder vans which travel around, searching out wireless sets. Not long ago, Jaguar had to escape over the roof tops with his wireless when he saw soldiers draw up in the square outside his apartment block. It took him a week to find a safe place to stay and Doreen and I were on duty the whole time until he came back on air.'

Eileen showed her how Jaguar would encode his messages, using a poem which had been agreed before he'd gone to France.

'He uses the Rudyard Kipling poem *If* to encode his messages.'

'Suppose the Germans find out? Won't they know how to decode all messages they intercept?' Genevieve asked.

'No, because each agent selects his own poem, so they're all different.'

Genevieve's roommate, Diana, was an experienced operator and offered to help her if she had any problems.

'I've got a new agent,' she told Genevieve. 'He's only been in France a fortnight although he's been out on a mission before. So far, he's keeping to his scheds, and long may that last! I don't know how those men can bear to go out to an occupied country. They're so brave.'

Genevieve didn't tell her she longed to be one of the agents dropped behind enemy lines!

It soon became apparent Diana was in awe of Genevieve, despite being more experienced.

'You're so slim,' Diana said, sighing

wistfully and looking down sadly at her round figure, 'And your hair is so glossy, how d'you get it like that?' she'd add, tugging a comb through her curly, ginger hair. 'I envy you so much, Genevieve!'

'But you have the most beautiful smile,' Genevieve told her, deflecting Diana's compliments. And it was true. When Diana smiled, her plain face lit up, making her quite pretty.

'D'you think so?' she asked doubtfully.

'Yes, definitely.'

'D'you think I need a bit of make-up?'

'Well, you don't need make-up, but I suppose it wouldn't hurt if you wanted to wear a little — '

'Only there's this chap I like, and . . . well, he doesn't seem to notice I exist. I wondered if perhaps I might try a bit of make-up and see if he notices me at the dance on Saturday. You wouldn't be a love and help me, would you? You've got such style. I bet all the

41

men'll be falling over themselves to dance with you.'

'Oh, I don't think so. I haven't had much luck in that direction in the past. I was very keen on one of the flight officers at Holsmere but he preferred my friend. And since then, I haven't had time to think about him or anyone else.'

★ ★ ★

The evening of the dance, Genevieve brushed Diana's hair, teasing out the curls and rolling it up into a sleek style, then she showed her how to apply some rouge and lipstick.

Diana turned her face from side to side, admiring her new look in the mirror, 'It's just a pity I'm built like a barrel, she said looking down at her middle.

'Just smile,' Genevieve said. 'You look so pretty, no one's going to be bothered to look anywhere other than your face.'

When they arrived at the dance,

Diana pointed out the man she liked, 'Donald Turner,' she said to Genevieve. 'Isn't he dreamy?'

Genevieve said that yes indeed he was dreamy, although she didn't like the look of him at all. He was handsome but he had a hard face and eyes which darted about, reminding her of a snake.

Victor Warrington, one of the operators who Genevieve had noticed always seemed to be hovering around Diana, came over to them.

'Can I get you ladies a drink?' he asked, not taking his eyes off Diana.

When he returned with their drinks, he asked Diana to dance and she agreed although she'd hardly taken her eyes off Donald. It was so obvious she wasn't interested in Victor, Genevieve was amazed he'd asked her to dance. Victor seemed a nice man and Genevieve couldn't understand why Diana hadn't noticed. Then again, affairs of the heart weren't exactly her strength.

While Diana and Victor were dancing, Genevieve was deep in thought, wondering if she could bring them together, when someone asked her to dance. It was Donald Turner. She could see why Diana was so smitten with the man. When he wanted to, he could turn on the charm — and he obviously wanted to now. She wasn't keen on dancing with him but it occurred to her that when he led her back to her seat, she could suggest he dance with Diana.

He pulled her close, pressing his body against hers and she tried to keep some distance between them, but not before Diana had spotted the two of them together. Immediately, she frowned and her eyes narrowed.

Genevieve reached behind her and stopped Donald's hand creeping from the curve of her back, downwards.

'What's the matter?' he asked.

'I'm not keen on your hands wandering over my body like that.'

'Oh, come on, loosen up a bit!' He

nibbled her ear and she pulled away.

'Please! Don't do that!'

'Why don't we go outside and I'll show you how to loosen up? We could go for a drive . . .'

'No, thank you.'

The number finished and Genevieve thanked him and pulled away.

'Come on!' he said, holding her arm tightly, 'The night's young.'

'Let me go!' she said, slipping free and making her way back to Diana.

'Diana, I don't know what you see in that man. He's ghastly!' Genevieve said, 'He simply can't take no for an answer. How arrogant!'

'You obviously led him on, Genevieve! I saw you snuggling up to him! You couldn't help yourself, could you?' said Diana angrily, 'The only man I wanted and you had to prove you could take him!'

'No, Diana, it wasn't like that! I was going to bring him over and suggest he dance with you!'

'So, where is he then?' Diana's words

were bitter, 'Be honest, you wanted him for yourself!'

Genevieve was about to say she'd refused to go for a drive with him but thought better of it. That wouldn't help the situation at all. She wondered if she ought to leave and let Diana calm down, when she saw Donald coming towards them.

'So,' he said, smiling at Genevieve, 'Who's your delightful friend?'

'My name's Diana.'

'Well, would you like to dance, Diana?'

'Oh, yes! Thank you, I would!'

As Donald led Diana to the dance floor, he glanced over his shoulder at Genevieve with a sardonic smile on his lips, as if to say *others want me even if you don't.*

What would Diana do when Donald held her too tightly? Genevieve knew she wasn't very experienced with men and hoped he would frighten her off. Perhaps then, Diana might realise what sort of man Donald was and the infatuation would be over.

However, Donald didn't hold her tightly, nor try to slide his hand down her back. He was very respectful and Genevieve wondered if it was because he also recognised Diana wasn't very experienced and was treating her carefully.

'Where's Diana?' It was Victor, and when he followed Genevieve's gaze and saw she was dancing, his face fell. 'That's Donald Turner,' he said, his voice bitter.

'Yes, he just danced with me and I couldn't wait for the number to finish. His hands were all over me. But he seems to be treating Diana with more respect.'

'That's typical!'

'What d'you mean?'

'He's only interested in one thing and he knows how to get it.'

'Yes, I guessed that. But surely Diana will see that too?'

'I'm not so sure,' Victor said.

They watched as the number ended

and Donald tucked Diana's arm under his and led her from the dance floor with a triumphant glance back.

'Where d'you think they're going?' Victor asked anxiously.

'Well, he asked me to go for a drive . . . '

'I think we ought to follow,' Victor said.

Genevieve hesitated. After all, Diana was a grown woman. Would she appreciate it if anyone followed her? It was obvious Victor really liked her and was jealous of the other man but if Diana wanted to go with Donald, she would be angry if Genevieve interfered.

'Well, if you're not coming, I'm going alone,' Victor said.

Genevieve reluctantly followed him outside.

They were in time to see Donald lead Diana to his car and hold the door open for her. Before he helped her in, he kissed her hand and they heard Diana gasp with pleasure.

'They're going for a drive,' Genevieve said, 'There's nothing we can do about that.'

'Yes, we can,' said Victor, 'We can follow at a distance.' He held up his car keys. 'Come on, follow me.'

'Oh, I don't know . . . ' said Genevieve aware she'd already upset Diana that evening.

'Come on!' said Victor, holding the door open for her and running around to the driver's seat.

He slowly backed out of his parking space and hung back until the other car had passed through the guarded entry and turned on to the road, then he followed at some distance so as not to make it obvious he was following. Victor rounded a bend but the road ahead was empty.

'We've lost them!' Genevieve said, not sure if she was alarmed or relieved.

'There's a turning here,' Victor said, 'If they're not down the lane, we definitely lost them.'

He swung the car round into the

narrow lane in time to see Donald pull over and stop.

Victor braked slightly and Genevieve was afraid he was going to stop as well and rush over to the car and drag Donald out. It was all very well being jealous but Donald and Diana were at liberty to do as they liked. To her relief, Victor glided past the parked car and kept going. As they passed, she peered into the car but it seemed the two people were merely talking. How furious Diana was going to be when she realised she and Victor had spied on her.

'Now what?' asked Genevieve.

'I don't know . . . Perhaps if I turn around and go past them again. If it all looks all right, then we'll go home. But if not . . . ' Having come this far, his plan made sense. 'It's too narrow to turn around,' Victor said, but then spotting the entrance to a farm he backed into it. By the time they returned to the parked car, Donald could be seen leaning nonchalantly against the bonnet, lighting a cigarette and Diana was some way off, walking along the road. He cupped his hand and shouted something to Diana. She briefly turned, shook her head and then increased her pace.

Victor accelerated towards her and she waved desperately, wanting to flag down a car — any car.

Victor pulled up beside Diana and wound down the window, 'Diana, are you all right?'

'Victor! Thank God!'

It was obvious she wasn't all right. There was enough moonlight to see her lipstick had been smudged across her face and most of the buttons torn off her shirt, and she was crying.

'Get in,' Victor said, 'We'll take you home.'

Genevieve sat in the back with her arms around the sobbing Diana while Victor drove to the base.

'He . . . he was hurting me, but I hit him and got away,' she sobbed. 'H-he said there was no point running off because I'd never find my way back home and . . . and I was so afraid!'

'Hush, hush, Diana. You weren't to know. Apparently, he has quite a reputation.'

'And with the three of us as witnesses, we might be able to stop him,' said Victor, 'I know other women have made complaints but he always manages to throw doubt on their accusations.'

★ ★ ★

Later, Diana made it clear she didn't want to complain about Donald. 'I feel so silly! It was my fault. After all, I didn't have to go with him.'

'It wasn't your fault at all! And if you don't say anything, he'll simply pick on someone else. And Victor was there. They'll take the word of a man more readily than they will yours.'

'Victor . . . ' said Diana in a small voice. 'What must he think of me!'

'I'll tell you what he thinks of you,'

said Genevieve, 'He thinks you're wonderful.'

'I'm sure he can't.'

'It was he who insisted we follow you to make sure you were all right.'

'Did he?'

'Yes, he obviously thinks very highly of you.'

'We've always been friends. We started working here at the same time. But I didn't know he was interested in me.' She paused for a moment, then added, 'But he won't be now. Not after my disgraceful behaviour. And what's more, I'm amazed you're still speaking to me.'

'Your behaviour wasn't disgraceful at all. It was Donald Turner who behaved atrociously. You did nothing wrong. I'm sure Victor feels the same.'

'Well, that's very generous of you to say so but I'm sure if Victor ever felt anything for me, he doesn't now.'

'Why don't you talk to him — '

'Heavens above! I'd be too embarrassed!'

'But you'll have to see him when we report Donald. You've got to talk to him sometime.'

'I . . . I'm not sure I'm going to report Donald . . . I think I'd rather forget the whole thing.'

'Look,' said Genevieve, 'I've got a shift now but let's go for a walk after lunch and discuss it. Shall we say one thirty at the summer house? We'll just go for a stroll.'

'All right, if you think so. But I'm not sure you'll change my mind about reporting Donald.'

At quarter past one, Genevieve arrived at the wooded area next to the sunken garden and hid among the trees. At twenty-five minutes past one she saw Diana approach the summer house and go inside. She checked her watch.

One twenty-eight.

Victor came striding across the lawn to the summer house, checking his watch.

Genevieve held her breath, hoping Diana wouldn't storm out, realising

54

she'd been tricked.

One thirty-five.

Diana and Victor were still inside.

One forty-five.

Genevieve decided it was time to go back to her room. Her plan appeared to have worked and if nothing more developed between them, well, at least they were talking.

Just as Genevieve was about to leave the cover of the trees, Diana and Victor came out of the summer house deep in conversation. Not wanting to be seen and to disrupt whatever was going on between them, Genevieve turned and headed into the sunken garden, realising too late they were headed in that direction too. Even worse, she knew there was only one entrance, so she wouldn't be able to leave without them seeing her . . . unless she scrambled up the wall and jumped down the other side. Luckily, the wisteria growing up the wall was sturdy and held her weight as she climbed, making it to the top as Diana and Victor reached the entrance.

'Heavens above, Genevieve! Whatever have you done to your face?' Diana asked when she got back to their room later, 'And your arms!'

Genevieve explained what had happened and how she'd escaped over the wall.

'Ouch!' Diana said, 'Fancy not checking what you were jumping on to.'

'There wasn't time. You were both walking fast, so I took a chance.'

'I've got some Calamine lotion if you want. It's good for stinging nettle rash. It's very soothing.'

'Yes please, my cheeks and arms feel like they're on fire!'

Diana began to laugh, 'I should really be cross with you for tricking me, but actually, Victor was so nice and being alone in the summer house with him gave us time to talk. So, thank you.'

Genevieve dabbed her face with Calamine lotion and smiled. The stinging and itching would be worth it if Diana and Victor were friends again, or perhaps even became more than friends.

'Just promise me one thing,' Diana said. 'Don't give up the day job. You might be an expert wireless operator and godmother but despite all the secrets, you'll never make an agent!'

Genevieve knew Diana was teasing since she'd never told her about her dream of serving in France, so she laughed at her friend's joke. But she was disappointed in herself, thinking, *What sort of agent d'you think you'd make? You were almost trapped by the people you were tailing!*

★ ★ ★

'Genevieve, would you be a dear?' Diana asked, 'I've just heard I've got to go on duty immediately. We've received a message to say Minotaur's missing, so Pauline and I will have to share the duty until further notice. I was supposed to be going out with Victor,

57

but can you let him know I won't be able to meet him, please?'

Victor was disappointed when Genevieve told him Diana was on duty until Pauline took over at midnight — unless her agent, Minotaur sent a message — but Victor knew what was at stake and walked back to the main house with her.

Genevieve was still awake when Diana got back to their room. 'Minotaur made contact, thankfully. There was a fault on his radio but he's fixed it now. Hopefully tomorrow, he'll keep to his usual sched time.'

'I told Victor you had to work and he said he'd try to see you tomorrow,' Genevieve said.

'He was waiting when I finished and walked me back. Oh Genevieve, he's such a lovely man. Fancy waiting all that time for me to finish!'

'I'm so glad.'

'You know, I didn't think I'd be able to hold my head up after I was so stupid about Donald Turner, but

58

Victor's been marvellous. And I'm so pleased Donald got into trouble!'

'I'm pleased some good came out of it,' said Genevieve turning out her light and pulling the covers up.

'However long the storm may last, however dark the sky, the sun will once again return, on that you can rely,' said Diana, climbing into bed.

'What did you say?' Genevieve snapped the light back on and sat up.

Diana looked startled, 'What's the matter? It's just a few lines of a poem I know, that's all.'

'Yes,' persisted Genevieve, 'How does it go?

'However long the storm may last, however dark the sky, the sun will once again return, on that you can rely. Do you know it?

'Yes,' Genevieve said, not mentioning it was her mother's poem. 'But where did you learn it?'

'It's the poem my agent chose to encode his messages. Why are you looking at me like that?'

'Sorry. I learned it a long time ago. It took me by surprise. D'you know the rest of it?'

'Yes . . . A rainbow is a promise that's painted in the sky, assurance that the greyest clouds are merely passing by. However long the storm may last, however dark the sky, The sun will once again return, on that you can rely,' said Diana, 'I don't know if there's any more. That's the only part I know. How funny you know it, too. Before I had to learn it, I'd never heard of it and I've no idea who wrote it. Have you?'

Genevieve shook her head. She couldn't speak! The poem was only known to her family, so that could only mean one thing . . . Minotaur must be the code name for JP!

She shivered. JP's godmother was Diana. Of course, she'd known he was out in France but this confirmation made it so real. And if there was any doubt about the poem, the code name he'd chosen confirmed his identity. Genevieve's pet nickname for JP was

60

Miney which had come from the name Minotaur. Years ago, the family had been staying in her grandfather's château and she and JP had discovered one of the many caves which were plentiful in the area. JP suggested they play at being Theseus and the Minotaur.

'You can be Theseus and I'll be the Minotaur. You go and hide and I'll hunt you,' he'd said.

When JP left her in the black, echoing cavern, Genevieve had been frightened and having no idea who Theseus nor the Minotaur were, she'd screamed when JP had leaped at her, roaring! She'd run terrified from the cave back to her mother and told her that JP was being a Miney-Tore and she didn't like it.

'Are you going to turn the light out, Genevieve?' Diana asked, looking at her roommate quizzically.

'Oh, yes of course!' She wouldn't let Diana know she knew the identity of her agent.

Secrecy was maintained at every level on the listening and transmission station — the fewer people who knew the identity or location of agents, the safer the men in the field would be. And she didn't want to risk getting Diana in trouble for unwittingly giving away a secret.

★ ★ ★

Three days later, Diana was back on twenty-four-hour duty, sharing with her counterpart, Pauline.

'What's happened to Minotaur?' Genevieve asked as casually as she could.

'He missed his scheds. And we've had a report from a different agent that his group's been infiltrated by the Gestapo. Several people have been arrested.'

Genevieve turned away and pretended to tie her shoelace in case Diana saw her eyes brim and tears slip down her cheeks.

While Diana was working with Pauline around the clock, Genevieve knew her brother was in danger — possibly even in prison. Possibly even . . .

No! She dared not think of her brother being anything other than alive and well.

After a few days, radio confirmation was received that several of the agents who'd been with Minotaur had, indeed, been arrested by the Gestapo and were imprisoned in Fresnes Prison, just south of Paris. But no one knew where Minotaur was.

Genevieve felt sick with fear and the only way she could take her mind off her worry was to throw herself into her work.

* * *

'Some top brass from HQ are coming today,' Diana told Genevieve as they ate breakfast.

'How do you know?'

63

'Victor told me. They're doing an inspection, so make sure your uniform's neat and tidy.'

'My uniform is always neat and tidy!'

Genevieve had just finished her shift when a FANY sergeant appeared and summoned her to Captain Harvey's office. 'You're wanted immediately,' he said.

When Genevieve entered the office, Captain Harvey introduced her to Major O'Grady, a senior member of SOE.

'Miss Lawrence, I understand when you started working for SOE, you expressed a desire to work undercover in France.'

'Yes, sir.'

'And have you changed your mind?'

'No, sir!'

'Good, good . . . Well, SOE policy has recently changed. We are considering sending women behind enemy lines, you see, and if you'd like to be interviewed, we'd be happy to see if you are the right sort of material.'

'I would very much like to try, sir.'

Major O'Grady beamed. 'Jolly good show.'

He made it clear that although she'd been selected for interview, it didn't mean she'd necessarily make it to France. Even if she was accepted, there would be many tests and courses over several months and if at any stage she failed or wanted to change her mind, there would be no dishonour and a new post would be found for her in a different department.

'You realise, of course, that women in the Army, Navy and Royal Air Force are barred from any armed combat . . .'

'Yes, sir.'

'Recently, someone managed to find a loophole. The First Aid Nursing Yeomanry Corps, as you know, is a civilian organisation. It's on the Army list but the beauty of it is, it's not actually part of the Army and therefore not subject to the rules governing the services. That means SOE can deploy

FANYs as armed agents and it cannot be deemed to be breaching any statutes . . .

'You've gone pale at the mention of deploying FANYs as armed agents, Miss Lawrence. Now is the time to say if that is not acceptable to you. It would be quite understandable, and if so, you'll be able to carry on your work here at the station with no black mark against your name.' He looked at her over the top of his glasses and waited for her reply.

'I will do whatever it takes, sir. And if that means being armed, I'm happy to do so,' she said, angry with herself for blanching at the thought of carrying a gun.

'And *use* them?'

'Yes, sir,' she said with determination.

Major O'Grady chewed his pipe thoughtfully. 'Well, Miss Lawrence, in that the case, do you have any objection to joining FANY?'

'No, sir.'

'You realise that under the Geneva

Convention, there's no provision for the protection of women prisoners of war, so if you were caught, there's a great probability you'd be shot as a spy?'

'Yes, sir.'

'Excellent, excellent. Well, there'll be a period of handover to a new godmother and then you'll join us to start your training at Wanborough.'

'Yes, sir! Thank you, sir!'

Over the next few weeks, Genevieve joined the FANY, exchanging her blue uniform for one of khaki and was promoted to Ensign. Then, she handed over her scheds with Jaguar to a new godmother and after saying goodbye to Diana, Victor and the other friends she'd made, she travelled to Wanborough Manor, near Guildford.

2

The girl sitting at the desk next to Genevieve smiled, 'It seems like you and I are the only women here,' she said, looking at the men seated at the rows of desks arranged one behind the other as if set out for a school exam. 'I'm Nathalie, Nathalie Rochefort.' She extended her hand across the aisle between the desks.

'Genevieve Lawrence.' She shook her hand.

'I expect we'll be roommates,' Nathalie said, 'They can't put us in with any of the men.'

'Silence please,' the instructor said, 'You have one hour to complete the assessment. You may begin now.'

Nathalie smiled and mouthed *Good luck*.

The two girls were indeed roommates and immediately struck up a friendship. Like Genevieve, Nathalie had one French and one English parent although it was her father who was French and her mother English. She also spoke the two languages fluently.

Nathalie was slightly taller than Genevieve although both girls were slim and physically fit. They weren't as fast as the men on the obstacle courses and cross country runs but were both determined to keep up. Their dedication paid off because after three weeks, they both passed and were told to prepare to go to the Highlands of Scotland for the next part of their training.

Several of the men on their course dropped out, although no one knew if they'd left voluntarily or simply failed, but it gave the girls confidence that they'd competed with a group of men and succeeded. The girls travelled on the train to Scotland with the men who'd become friends.

Eric Vandevelde was a French-speaking Belgian who'd fled to England when the Germans marched into his country and he'd volunteered to help support the Resistance Movement in either Belgium or France. He was tall and athletic, unlike his friend Tom Drummond, who'd struggled with all the physical tests but had excelled at everything else. The third man was Peter Vidal, a French-speaking Canadian who'd been living and working in England when war broke out.

Nathalie had admitted to Genevieve she might be falling for Peter but as yet, he hadn't expressed an interest in her. 'It's probably just as well,' Nathalie said resignedly, 'Now's not a good time to fall in love, with us all about to go to France . . . who knows what's going to happen?'

Genevieve knew she was right but couldn't help noticing how her friend's eyes sparkled whenever she was with Peter.

Eric made it clear he was keen on Genevieve but she'd wanted to put all her energy into her training and tests. He was handsome and good company but somehow, her heart wasn't in it.

'What's wrong with him?' Nathalie asked noticing his interest in Genevieve, 'He's good looking and he's obviously smitten with you!'

'There's nothing wrong with him at all . . . I just . . . I don't feel anything other than friendship. I don't want to give him false hope. It's not fair.'

Nevertheless, the group of five got on remarkably well together and the journey to Scotland passed quickly.

Training at Wanborough Manor had tested their physical and psychological abilities to discover if they were suitable to become agents. Having shown they were capable, they moved on to several weeks of paramilitary training. Their instructors were mainly battle-hardened men who'd returned from Dunkirk. They taught their recruits weapon-handling, field craft, the use of explosives and other methods of demolition and sabotage. The only skill that worried Genevieve was silent killing. It was bad enough thinking about aiming a gun at someone and pulling the trigger but quite another using one's bare hands to take someone's life.

'I suppose,' Nathalie said with a sigh, 'if I'm ever in the position where it's him or me and the only weapon I have is my hands, I'll use them.'

Genevieve secretly hoped she'd never find herself in that situation but she knew how dangerous her life would be now. So, as they were advised to do, they repeatedly made small chopping motions with the soft part of their hands against tables and chairs, to harden them up.

Ironically, one of the things that frightened Nathalie most was the thought of the dentist.

'I hate the dentist! And I've got several fillings!' she wailed, knowing they'd been done by an English dentist and the silver fillings would have to be replaced by gold ones like those used in France. Genevieve had a few but they'd been done in France so didn't need hers replaced.

Everything, they discovered, had to be carried out in the French manner. Their trainers ensured they ate their meals, used the telephone, greeted each other with kisses on each cheek, summoned a waiter, all exactly as a French person would do.

At first, Genevieve wondered if such attention to detail was really necessary. Surely a Gestapo agent wouldn't notice whether she combed her hair in the French fashion? But they were told about an agent who'd arrived in France and had been on her way to a safe house. When she crossed a busy road. She'd looked the wrong way for traffic, stepped out, and nearly been run over. Unfortunately, she'd been spotted by a Gestapo agent who'd shrewdly guessed why she'd looked the wrong way and arrested her. She'd been caught after less than twenty-four hours on French soil. After that, Genevieve paid more attention. If her life depended on those tiny details, it was worth taking note and acting on the advice.

As the training progressed, the five friends bonded in a way which would not have occurred under normal circumstances. Those who found they were most able in certain subjects helped those less able. Nathalie and Genevieve, with their nimble fingers, were able to strip, clean and reassemble guns faster than the men but Peter and Eric excelled at hand-to-hand combat. Tom's strength was in anything to do with radios so it seemed likely he would be a wireless operator.

They were shown how a handful of sugar or sand in a fuel tank could disable a car and which ingredients could be easily acquired in a pharmacy and then carefully mixed to make explosives. With their knowledge of cookery, the girls were better at this than the men because they were more meticulous at weighing the ingredients.

Each night, all the trainees dined, in full uniform, in the Officers' Mess. It might appear that the training and observation of the recruits was over for the day but that was not so. They were scrutinised to ensure they were eating and behaving as if they were French. Wine and spirits were freely available and their consumption was encouraged because it was important the conducting officers knew all the students could hold their drink. An agent who started to speak in English when drunk would soon be apprehended! And anyone who talked too freely could incriminate themselves and those associated with them.

Genevieve had a good tolerance to alcohol and found she could drink a lot without it affecting her. Not so Nathalie, whose head started to spin after a few whiskys. But at least she merely fell asleep and didn't behave in a way that might endanger herself or her comrades, or she would have been dismissed and on her way home. After a riotous night drinking, Genevieve woke up as fresh as usual and was able to recall the hilarity of the previous evening but Nathalie always nursed a hangover and felt wretched until lunch time.

On the day they were to start a course where they slept out and lived off the land, Nathalie wasn't sure she'd be able to cope. 'I'm sick,' she said, pulling the blankets over her head.

'Come on, get up or you'll be late. You know they hate it if we're not on time.'

'Honestly, Genevieve, tell them I'm sick.'

'They'll know it's a hangover. They were watching last night. No one's going to believe you're sick! You must pass this course.'

'Tell them I've got food poisoning.'

'Don't be ridiculous! If you'd got food poisoning, so would the rest of us. Come on! Peter, Tom and Eric are all waiting downstairs.'

'Oh! I can't bear the thought of hiking. My head's thumping!'

'I'll get you an aspirin. You can't give up now. We've been through so much and you know your hangover'll be gone in a few hours.'

'Shhh!' said Nathalie, 'You're shouting and it's splitting my head!'

Genevieve got ready quickly and went downstairs to find the others. She asked Peter if he'd go and get her out of bed, knowing she'd be more likely to try harder if he was there. Ten minutes later, Peter and a very fragile-looking Nathalie came downstairs.

'No time for breakfast I'm afraid,' Tom said.

'I couldn't face anything.'

'Hmm, you'll be hungry later,' Eric said, shaking his head anxiously. Of the five of them, Eric was the most practical. 'You know we won't eat a proper meal until Tuesday.'

'Good!' Nathalie said, with a toss of her head, 'Now will people please stop talking about food and let's get going. I've been dragged from my bed by this monster,' she placed her hand on Peter's arm, 'and if I've got to do this, I'd rather get it over and done with as soon as possible!'

She kept her hand lightly resting on Peter's arm as they left the house and only removed it when they assembled outside with the other groups ready to be dismissed.

'So, you've finally decided to join us,' said the instructor to a ripple of laughter from the others. He told each group their itinerary and warned them there would be checkpoints on their routes to ensure no one cheated — although they would all be miles from any towns or villages.

'That was a clever trick, using Peter to get me out of bed,' Nathalie said later as they set off.

'Trick?' Genevieve said innocently, 'I'm sure I don't know what you mean!'

'You know how much I like him, don't you?' Genevieve nodded. 'Do I make it that obvious?'

'Not to anyone else, don't worry.'

'Thank goodness. I want to pass this course more than anything and to go to France, so I've fought against liking

Peter, but I just can't help myself. The more I get to know him, the more I'm attracted to him. But for all I know, he only thinks of me as a friend. Every so often, I think he really does like me, and at others there doesn't seem to be anything there at all.'

'He may be afraid the conducting officers wouldn't like it if two of their would-be agents become romantically involved. It's only recently they've accepted women on this course and I've notice a jibe or a look from one of the other men that tells me we're not really accepted.'

'You may be right. Peter's so committed to passing this course, I don't think he'd let anything get in the way. If we're both sent to France we may never meet again,' Nathalie said sadly. 'Anyway, on a happier note,' she added, 'the aspirin and the fresh air have got rid of my headache. On a less happy note, I'm starving!'

'Oh, Nathalie! Honestly!'

'I brought a little something in case I

was hungry later" she said with a laugh.

'We're not supposed to have any food.'

'Yes, but I didn't have breakfast, so I'm going to need something to keep going.' She reached inside her jacket and fumbled with her shirt buttons. 'I tucked a bar of chocolate in my bra,' she said pulling it out. 'Oh! I think it's melted.'

'For goodness sake, don't show the others,' Genevieve said. 'You know we're supposed to pool any food we find and share it out.'

Nathalie opened the wrapper gingerly and surreptitiously licked the melted chocolate.

'What's this?' said Peter, who'd come up silently behind the girls. 'Eating, are you?'

Nathalie licked her lips to ensure there wasn't any tell-tale chocolate and shook her head.

'Stop, a minute,' said Peter. He held her chin and leaned close to her, rubbing his nose against hers, then briefly kissed her lips. Nathalie was surprised but didn't resist as he kissed her more passionately. She closed her eyes and melted towards him just as he broke away.

'I knew it!' he said triumphantly, 'You've been eating chocolate! I can taste it on your lips!'

'You beast!' said Nathalie, realising he'd only kissed her to check. Not only had he discovered she'd lied about eating but must surely know how much she liked him. He knew her well enough to realise she'd rebuff unwanted advances. And she'd just shown him if he chose to kiss her, she'd willingly comply!

'I'm such an idiot!' she said to Genevieve once Peter strode off to the other two men.

'Well, at least now, he definitely knows how you feel, chérie.'

'That's true . . . so if he continues to hold me at arm's length, I'll know he doesn't feel the same.'

★   ★   ★

It was almost dark by the time they reached the forest and found a camp site. They built a shack for the night out of branches, then made a fire and set some traps for rabbits.

'Turnips?' Nathalie said, 'That's dinner?'

'Oh, don't make such a fuss. You knew what the deal was when you signed up with SOE. With any luck we'll have rabbit tomorrow, but on tonight's menu, it's wild turnips I'm afraid,' Peter said, turning to take the ones he'd dug up down to the river to wash. 'Anyway, I don't know what you're complaining about, I seem to remember you ate a whole bar of chocolate earlier today,' he added with a laugh.

Nathalie blushed.

'By the way, it was delectable,' he said, 'I might have to kiss you again just to check you're not concealing more chocolate bars!'

Genevieve was just returning from the river, having washed the wild turnips she'd found, and saw Nathalie's blush and Peter's smile. There was definitely a spark there, she decided.

That night, after eating the wild turnip leaves and roots, the three men and two women huddled in their blankets under the branch shelter they'd built and Genevieve noted that Peter had contrived to lie next to Nathalie all night.

They set off early the next morning and Nathalie walked with Peter.

'They're getting very friendly,' said Eric, falling into step beside Genevieve.

'I know. I'm not sure it's wise. The course'll be finished soon and then we'll all be sent to France. We all know the life expectancy of an agent.'

'Yes,' he said, 'it's pitifully short. But perhaps that's why it's a good thing they get together now. If they've only got a short while to live, they might as well grab some happiness while they can.'

'I hadn't thought of it like that,' she said.

'And since we're on the subject of romance and the prospect of a short life, Genevieve, I've a confession to make . . . '

'Oh? That sounds serious.'

'I probably wouldn't have said anything if it hadn't been for Nathalie and Peter but . . . well, it's just that . . . well, I like you . . . very much.'

'You do?' Genevieve feigned surprise.

Nathalie, Peter, Tom and Eric had all become good friends. They'd been through so much together and their shared intentions had bonded them in a way that wouldn't have happened during normal times. Knowing they were unlikely to be alive by the end of the year had given their experiences together an intensity that Genevieve hadn't expected. Nevertheless, romance was a complication she didn't need. And now, Eric was telling her he had feelings for her.

'I can see I've surprised you,' Eric said. 'Or perhaps it's just that you don't feel the same about me . . . ' he stopped sadly.

'No, Eric, it's not that. I think you're jolly wonderful. But I was focusing on going to France and I . . . well, I'm not sure I . . .'

'No need to finish,' Eric said. 'I can see you don't feel the same. But I'll not give up on you, old girl. If there's one thing I've learned on this course it's to persevere and to use my initiative — '

'That's two things,' she said with a smile.

'That's what I love most about you,' he said. 'Your sense of humour.'

Tom, who was behind the two couples called out, 'Oi, you four, you're going in the wrong direction!' He was staring at his compass and pointing to their left. 'It's this way.'

That night, as they slept side by side, keeping each other warm beneath the makeshift wooden shelter, Genevieve thought about Eric's confession. He was probably right about grabbing what little happiness they could in the time they had left and that appeared to be what Nathalie and Peter were doing as they were now snuggled up next to each other.

Genevieve was lying between Nathalie and Tom, Eric on the other side of Tom. He'd deliberately not taken the opportunity to be next to her and she wasn't sure if it was because she'd not shown any enthusiasm for his declaration or because he didn't want to rush her. He was such a considerate man, she thought it was probably the latter. Why didn't she feel the same about him as he felt about her? It didn't make sense. But when had love ever made sense?

Their group was the first to return to base — hungry, wet, dirty and tired — but they'd beaten the other groups and all received excellent marks for their survival course.

Nathalie and Peter were discreet — after all, they'd been trained to live unobtrusively and to evade detection. Genevieve began to spend more time with Eric, wondering if she was being unkind in allowing him to think she'd fall in love with him as he'd done with her. Yet if she didn't spend time with him, how would she know? Nevertheless, she could tell that whatever she felt for Eric — and she definitely liked him a lot — she didn't feel the same about him as Nathalie felt about Peter.

★ ★ ★

The five friends successfully finished their training in Scotland and after meeting with the commanding officer who gave them their reports and congratulated them individually, they were sent to an airfield at Ringway, near Manchester, to take part in a three-day course in parachuting.

'This is the bit I'm dreading,' said Genevieve, 'I'm not sure how I'm going to cope. Suppose I get up in the aircraft and then can't jump?'

'Everyone's nervous,' said Eric, taking her hand, 'even if they don't admit it. But you'll be fine. We'll all encourage each other.'

Genevieve let her hand remain in Eric's. It was comforting and gave her strength.

'Arm forward, curved to break your fall! Keep your knees together! Now, roll as you land! Roll!' the instructor bellowed, as they repeatedly practised the correct landing technique. Finally, when he was certain they would be able to land safely, they were sent up in aircraft at night.

'I thought I'd be terrified dropping out of a plane at night,' Nathalie shouted above the noise of the aircraft engine. 'But on reflection, I think it might be worse during the day. At least I can't see anything so it's not as frightening as I thought.'

Genevieve had a moment of panic over the opening through which she'd drop. Eric had already advised her to keep her eyes on the face of the sergeant who'd give her the signal to jump and to step forward without looking down.

'Go!' the sergeant yelled, bringing

down his raised arm in case there was any doubt.

The wind suddenly snatched her, taking her breath away and then she was falling . . . falling until her parachute opened with a jerk and billowed above. Then, she was floating down but the ground seemed to be racing towards her.

Arm forward! Knees together! Roll! She told herself as she hit the ground. Dazed, she sat up.

She'd survived — and nothing was broken!

Above her, she could see ghostly parachutes at various heights hanging in the night sky as the others completed their first parachute drop. Several of the other recruits hadn't been able to jump and had packed their bags and left Ringway. Tom had almost not made it, having refused to jump until Eric urged him on. Once he'd done his first drop, he'd managed the other two.

Having successfully completed the required three jumps, the five friends were sent to the undercover agent finishing school in Beaulieu, near the New Forest. It was here the trainees learned the craft of espionage as well as a great deal about the enemy. They needed to identify Germans by their uniform and rank insignia, and Luftwaffe aircraft by their silhouette, as well as how to survive a Gestapo interrogation.

'If you're captured, you must attempt to keep silent for at least twenty-four hours, it'll give your fellow agents a chance to escape,' the instructor told them, 'Of course forty-eight hours would be even better,' he added.

One night after the girls had gone to bed, Genevieve was awoken by a hand over her mouth! She struggled to free herself but was quickly overpowered, gagged and tied hand and foot. She'd known that during their time in Beaulieu, each agent would be put through a simulated interrogation but she hadn't imagined anything as realistic as this! In fact, it was so real it was hard to believe the men who were dragging her to the basement weren't German, especially as they were dressed in Gestapo uniforms. She was taken to a bare, damp room where she was tied to a chair, a bright light was shone into her face.

'My name is Genevieve Lawrence and I'm a French citizen,' she repeated over and over in response to the men's questioning. They shouted, slapped her and repeatedly fired questions but she gave the same response, telling them nothing, becoming increasingly exhausted as the hours passed, sagging in the chair and held upright only by her bonds.

I will not give in. I will tell them nothing.

At last, the bright light shining in her eyes was turned off and the single light bulb overheard was switched on. Major O'Grady entered the dingy room with a cup of tea.

'Jolly good show, Miss Lawrence. First class.'

She was bemused to see the men in

Gestapo uniforms untie her as the major give her the tea.

'Let's hope you don't have to experience anything like that for real, Miss Lawrence, but if you do, you are obviously brave enough to withstand interrogation, at least long enough to allow your fellow agents to escape. Congratulations.'

Nathalie had been taken the same evening and had undergone similar treatment in another room in the basement. She too had not cracked under the pressure. The girls were sworn to secrecy and not allowed to warn anyone, but having both had the same ordeal could discuss it together.

'I had no idea it would be so terrifying!' Nathalie said, 'It seemed so real!'

'I know,' said Genevieve. 'Well, that's incentive to put everything we've learned about evading the Gestapo into practice. I never want to go through anything like that again!'

★ ★ ★

The large group of men Genevieve and Nathalie started training with months before decreased as trainees dropped out, either when they found a certain part of the course was unacceptable, such as the unarmed combat or parachuting, or when they were incapable of reaching the high enough standard set by the instructors. By the end of the course, Genevieve, Nathalie, Tom, Eric and Peter all passed with excellent marks.

'Well done, everyone,' Peter said, 'Now, we're going to do as Mr Churchill urged the SOE to do and set Europe ablaze!'

⋆ ⋆ ⋆

They travelled to London, to Orchard Court and after waiting in the same bathroom for a short time, each attended a debriefing meeting with the head of F Section, Major Buckmaster, who read out their report and congratulated them on completing the course.

He told them they were to go to Buckinghamshire to await orders and to become familiar with their new identities — all except Tom, who was to leave for France as soon as possible.

That night, they arranged to meet in the Wentworth Club in Mayfair to celebrate their achievements and to say goodbye to Tom. After being schooled in his new identity, he was due to fly out two days later.

The others knew they wouldn't have to wait much longer before they left on their own missions. It was unlikely any of them would be on English soil by the end of the month.

Each of them was aware it was probably be the last time they'd all be together.

Eric whistled when he picked Genevieve up and saw her in her blue gown.

'I've never seen you in anything other than uniform and overalls, with mud all over your face,' he said, holding her hand above her head and making her twirl around. 'You're so beautiful,

Genevieve,' he said with tears in his eyes, 'I'm not sure I'm going to be able to bear this evening.'

She knew what he meant. The five of them had become so close they felt as if they were more tightly bonded than family and being wrenched apart was going to be painful. Despite the gaiety of the night, it would be bittersweet.

Nathalie was also out of uniform, wearing a pale yellow dress and Peter couldn't take his eyes off her. 'I'm almost tempted to steal you away and forget all about SOE,' he said.

'Don't you dare! We didn't go through all that torture to give up on our chances to go to France . . . although,' she added with a sly smile, 'it's mighty tempting!'

They all drank heavily, trying to forget about the future, except Tom who wanted to keep a clear head because in the early hours, he'd have to leave for the airfield on his way to France.

Each network, or circuit, as they were

known, had an organiser in charge, couriers who ran messages between circuits, and — arguably the most important — the wireless operator, without whom there was no communication with London.

The instructors on their course had found Tom to be the best wireless operator they'd ever encountered and when one of the circuits had lost their man, it was decided Tom would be sent as speedily as possible to replace him.

Nathalie and Peter had eyes only for each other and by midnight, they'd disappeared, leaving the other three on their own. Genevieve suspected they'd gone back to Nathalie's room but didn't mind. She envied their total absorption in each other. So she felt it her duty to make sure Tom didn't feel left out and danced with him and Eric, insisting the three of them remain together until Tom had to go, despite his protests that she and Eric should spend time together.

She knew Eric was disappointed they

weren't alone but neither would he want to make Tom feel as if he was being pushed out. If she was honest, she wasn't sure she wanted to be alone with Eric.

After Tom said goodbye and left, Genevieve danced with Eric and as the music in the club slowed and the mood became more romantic, the couples who remained on the dance floor melted into each other after the energy of the earlier numbers.

Genevieve and Eric danced cheek-to-cheek and moved as one around the dance floor. She could feel the beating of his heart and wondered why she hadn't suggested they go off together like Nathalie and Peter. What was wrong with her? Eric was such a lovely man — handsome, kind, loyal and loving — what more could a girl ask?

She decided she'd have to get over her stupid reticence and let him know that he was very special to her before it was too late and they were parted . . . perhaps forever.

He walked her home, through the London streets and took her up to her room, then kissed her. It was time to ask him in. *Now! Do it now!* But the words simply wouldn't come.

'Genevieve . . . d'you think I . . . well, d'you think I might come in?' he asked uncertainly.

She stared at him for a second and before she could force herself to say yes, he leaned forward and kissed her on the tip of the nose.

'Don't say anything, chérie. Your silence has told me all I need to know.'

'Oh Eric!'

She tightened her arms around his neck and held him but he gently peeled her hands away and stepped back, with a sad smile.

'I love you, Genevieve,' he said, then turned and left her at the door.

★ ★ ★

Eric didn't mention what had happened after their evening at the

98

Wentworth Club. Or more correctly, what hadn't happened. He behaved like a perfect gentleman and Genevieve had been grateful for his thoughtfulness, even if she did catch him watching her wistfully from time to time as they spent the next few days at a large house in Buckinghamshire, being given their new identities and orders.

They were tested repeatedly to check they were completely familiar with their new names, identities and life histories.

'My code name is Heart,' said Genevieve, 'My field name is Angelique and the name on my official identity papers is Mademoiselle Odette Raymonde. I am twenty-years old. I am single and I rent a room in the doctor's house where I work as a receptionist. My parents died in a road accident five years ago and I have no siblings . . .'

The code name was the name by which SOE would refer to her, and the field name was what she'd be called by her fellow agents in France.

Nathalie's code name was Cinnamon

and her field name Estelle.

'Your names and details must come as naturally to you as if you were born with them,' the instructor said, questioning Genevieve again on which school she'd attended and where her parents were buried.

Eric and Peter had already left for France and Nathalie was very subdued since they'd gone.

'I don't think I can bear it,' she said.

'Are you thinking of pulling out?' Genevieve asked in alarm.

'Certainly not! What would be the good of staying in England on my own? I want to do my bit to fight the Nazis. As soon as the war's over, Peter and I'll be together, but first we have to win.'

Genevieve's heart was heavy. The likelihood of both her friends coming back to England was slim. It occurred to her that rather than their love being an unwelcome distraction, perhaps it would make them doubly determined to succeed as SOE agents. After all, she was driven by love too — love for her brother, JP, and she too was resolute she was going to survive and if possible, find out what happened to him.

'If the weather is suitable on Friday, Heart and Cinnamon will be flying out at twenty-two hundred hours to a dropping point near Orleans,' the instructor said. You will be met by a welcoming committee and then taken to separate safe houses. Heart, you will join the Tulip Circuit. Cinnamon, you will join the Monarch Circuit. You will both act as couriers within those circuits . . . '

The details were repeated until the instructors were satisfied both girls had completely assumed their identities and were word perfect on plans.

*   *   *

Despite the heavy drizzle during Friday morning, the Met Office had forecast a fine, dry evening and with a full moon, conditions would be perfect for the flight across the Channel to France.

Genevieve packed her backpack with a few changes of clothes and her false identity papers. Everything she was taking had been checked by an expert to ensure they appeared to be French. British clothes labels were replaced with French labels, laundry tags were removed and any other tell-tale signs such as old receipts, loose change or bus tickets in pockets were taken away.

She'd attached the silver, heart-shaped charm that Sonny had given her to her watch bracelet and as everything she had was searched, she wondered if she'd be ordered to remove it. The watch was French — a gift from her parents which had been bought in Orleans, so she knew it would be allowed. But the charm?

It looked as though it had originally been part of the watch and after a momentary glance, the expert moved on to inspecting her handbag.

Inside the handbag were one million French Francs in notes to finance the

Tulip Circuit and the French Resistance and within the lining of the handbag, were concealed codes and ciphers, written on silk which were intended for the circuit's wireless operator, as well as the addresses of several safe houses and the passwords she'd need to make herself known to the owners.

Before the girls left, Vera Atkins, the Intelligence Officer for F Section came to see them off. She looked them up and down, nodded with satisfaction and then gave each of them a small gift of a silver compact.

'This is a keepsake to remind you wherever you are in France that you may be alone but we'll be thinking of you and will do our utmost to keep you safe. And if there's no alternative . . .' she tapped the button on the cuff of her shirt. Both girls knew exactly what she meant — concealed inside the buttons on their own cuffs were cyanide pills.

Miss Atkins nodded briefly and then turned on her heel, leaving the two newest SOE agents waiting to board their aircraft. They clung to each other silently, knowing that once aboard the Halifax bomber, there would be no time for goodbyes and that this might be the last time they saw each other.

* * *

Genevieve looked through the opening in the bottom of the plane to the dark shadows of the French landscape below. Far off, she could see the moonlight reflecting off the Loire River, lying like a silver ribbon draped across the ground. Wind whipped at the legs of her flying suit and she felt the rush of cold air hit her face as over the intercom, the pilot announced the dropping zone was ahead. They'd survived the heavy flak as they crossed the French coast but thankfully, they hadn't been bothered by the Luftwaffe, and now they'd almost reached their destination.

Genevieve checked her parachute

straps and took a deep breath, hoping her legs would obey her when it was time to drop into the void. Below, she saw a bonfire and torches indicating the landing area. The red light on the bulkhead switched to green. 'Go!'

Genevieve jumped.

The static line attached to her snapped taut, deploying the parachute, jerking her upwards as the canopy billowed and filled with air.

To her alarm, a stiff breeze caught her and despite tugging on the cord, she continued to veer away from the field with the bonfire. By the time she was about three hundred feet from the ground, she'd drifted off course and would be an easy target if there were any passing Germans. She was completely vulnerable and wouldn't stand a chance if anyone took a shot at her. And what if the party waiting for her on the ground weren't Tulip Circuit but Gestapo instead?

She would find out very soon.

Above, she saw Nathalie who'd

jumped seconds after her and about twenty other parachutes floating down, carrying boxes of guns, ammunition and plastic explosive as well as the valuable radio concealed in a suitcase.

Narrowly missing a small wood, Genevieve came down on the grass, remembering to keep her knees together and to roll until she stopped. She leaped to her feet, and pulled the release mechanism of her parachute, then gathered the silk fabric in her arms, ready to bury it.

Where was everyone? It was so dark she could see nothing, not even the bonfire she'd seen from the plane, although she could smell the smoke. She took the two pieces of spade from her backpack and, screwing them together, she started to dig a hole to bury the parachute as had been stressed during her training.

'Non! Non!' The voice came from behind her and she leapt with fright.

'I will take the parachute,' the man said, then when she turned around and her face was visible in the moonlight, he added, 'Mon Dieu! It's a girl!' Recovering from his shock, he added, 'Come with me.'

'I must bury the parachute,' she insisted.

'Non! There are too many uses for silk such as this! Burying it would be sacrilege,' the man said and took the bundle from her. 'Follow me, your friends are waiting for you.'

* * *

The man, who introduced himself as Marcel Pélissier, led her around the wooded area to a large field where the glowing embers of what had been a bonfire a short while ago could still be seen. Men moved silently like shadows over the field, gathering up parachutes and carrying boxes to a waiting truck.

'Follow me,' Marcel said, taking Genevieve to the man who appeared to be in charge, 'Here's the agent who drifted into the next field, Yves,' he said and hurried away to help load the last of the containers into the lorry.

'I'm Angelique,' Genevieve said.

Yves ran his hand through his hair and looked at her in horror, 'Another woman? Has London gone mad?'

That wasn't the welcome Genevieve expected.

'Where's Nathal — Estelle?' she said, angry with herself for forgetting Nathalie's field name.

'If you mean the other woman, she's already on her way to a safe house.'

'All loaded, boss,' Marcel said, running up to Yves, 'Let's go.'

Yves nodded at Genevieve, 'Get in the truck.'

No one spoke as the lorry sped along country lanes. There were too many boxes to conceal and if a German patrol stopped them, they would all be arrested. Most of the men had melted into the darkness once the truck was loaded, but Yves, leader of the Tulip Circuit, Marcel, a local resister, and the driver would all be seized — as well, of course, as Tulip's newest member, Angelique.

The truck swerved into a narrow, rutted track and pulled up sharply in front of a barn. A shadowy figure appeared and Marcel leaped from the truck to help him open the enormous doors then wave the truck into its cavernous interior. Once inside, the doors were closed and the driver turned off the engine, then he and Yves got out to join a group of waiting men. Genevieve followed but Yves signalled her to get out of the way.

'I can help,' she said in exasperation, guessing they were going to unload the crates.

'You can help best if you keep out of the way. The men'll be tripping over themselves to help you, if they see you. We don't need any delays. This is dangerous enough without calling Gallic chivalry into play.'

Genevieve stood back, watching the men unload the boxes and stack them at one end of the barn, then place bales of straw in front to conceal them — all except one box which contained the wireless inside the suitcase.

'Here, Henri — this one's for you!' one of the men shouted holding the suitcase high.

A chubby man ran forward to take the case and raised it to his lips, 'Lordy, lordy! A new wireless!'

He walked towards Genevieve and shook her hand, 'I'm Henri, the Tulip's wireless operator. So pleased to meet you.'

'I'm Angelique. I'm your courier. That's the first time since I've landed I've felt welcome.'

'Oh, don't mind Yves! He's got a lot on his mind — and we weren't expecting a girl.'

'Yes, I gathered that.'

'I imagine if London had mentioned they were sending a female operative, there might have been some resistance in the Resistance!' He laughed at his own joke and winked at her.

Genevieve thought she was going to

get on well with Henri — and it would be good to have a friend.

When all the boxes were hidden, the truck was driven away carrying most of the men, leaving Henri, Marcel, Yves and Genevieve.

Marcel took some bread and cheese out of his backpack and passed it around to the others who were sitting on bales of straw. Then he took out a bottle of wine and after withdrawing the cork, he wiped it with his sleeve and handed it to Genevieve to drink first.

'There's no point standing on ceremony, Marcel, Angelique'll have to get used to living rough. And if that means drinking out of the bottle after the men, so be it.'

'It doesn't bother me,' said Genevieve taking the bottle and drinking.

'By the way,' she said, 'you might not be happy London sent me but you'll be happy with this.' She took her handbag out of her backpack and opened it, tipping the French Francs onto the bale of straw. Then she slit the lining with a small knife and withdrew the silk fabric on which were the codes and ciphers which she passed to Henri.

'And you may also like this,' she said pulling out a bottle of whisky. 'Compliments of SOE.'

'Now you're talking!' said Henri taking the bottle from her, 'Although I'd better not have too much . . . ' he checked his watch, 'it's almost time for my sched.'

He ran his hands lovingly over the suitcase as he opened it, ready for transmission to London.

Genevieve wondered if she knew the godmother who'd be taking care of Henri's messages and wondered if by some chance it would be Diana. The thought of her former colleague working in Sevenoaks, straining to hear messages sent from places such as this barn, brought home the realisation that although the distance between them wasn't so great, they might as well have been on different sides of the universe.

With the aerial now in place, Henri

tuned in to the correct frequency and then asked for Genevieve's SOE code name.

'Heart,' she said.

Yves' eyes rolled and he shook his head in disbelief, 'Did you choose that code name?' She nodded. 'How very feminine and pretty,' he said.

'At least I've got a heart!' she snapped, 'And it's brave and true!'

Henri and Marcel burst out laughing and to Genevieve's surprise, even the corners of Yves' mouth twitched.

'She's got a point, old man,' said Henri. 'Now keep quiet, I'm about to get busy.' He checked his watch and after waiting a few seconds, he rapidly tapped on the key.

Yves beckoned Genevieve away from Henri, 'You must be tired. We'll all be sleeping up there . . . ' He pointed to a ladder which led up to a loft. 'Feel free to go at any time. I'm afraid you won't be sleeping in a bed for the next few nights, until all these guns have been picked up and I have time to take you

113

to your safe house.'

'No need to apologise,' Genevieve said, 'I'm used to sleeping rough.' It wasn't exactly true but she had survived the few days she'd spent with her friends sleeping out in the Scottish Highlands. A feeling of homesickness swept over her. Where were the others now? Were they even still alive?

She had the feeling Yves wanted to get rid of her and her instinct was to stay with him to find out why, but she was tired so she climbed the ladder into the loft and, keeping her flying suit on for warmth, lay down on the straw. Below, she heard the frantic tapping of Henri's morse key as he communicated with London and the low hum of men's voices in conversation. Whatever they were discussing, Yves had chosen to exclude her.

She shivered. There were gaps in the walls of the barn through which the cold wind whistled and she wondered how much sleep she'd get that night — and the next few nights — until she was taken to her safe house.

The ladder creaked telling her someone was coming into the loft. Instantly, she was wide awake. Marcel's head appeared.

'Here,' he said, climbing into the loft and throwing the parachute he'd prevented her from burying earlier. 'It's cold up here and you might need this.'

Genevieve gratefully took the silk canopy and laid part of it over her, spreading the rest of the fabric over the floor so that the men, when they finally came upstairs to sleep, would be able to use it too. She suspected that Yves might snub it, choosing instead to push it to one side, ignoring her gesture.

A short time later, she woke and realised the conversation and the tapping of Morse Code had ceased and had been replaced by gentle snoring all around her. Three figures lay together on the bales of straw at a respectful distance from her, and all of them under the parachute.

Monsieur Escoffier, the farmer who owned the barn arrived in the morning with ham, bread and coffee. Everyone ate hungrily and Genevieve noted the whisky she'd given them a few hours before was gone. So her gift at least had been welcome, even if she wasn't. She kept quiet, suspecting Yves would simply ignore her and carry on as if she wasn't there but to her surprise, over breakfast, he pointed to a bicycle which was leaning against the wall of the barn and told her she'd be busy that day, informing contacts that their guns and explosives were ready to be picked up — and the sooner, the better.

He handed her a sheet of paper with four contact names and addresses and a map.

'Marcel will go with you to the first check point. He's a postman, so he's well known by the Germans and is unlikely to be stopped. Once you get through — assuming you're not picked up by the guards — you'll be on your own. It's quite a long ride but you should be back by nightfall,' he said in a tone which suggested he thought she probably couldn't even ride a bicycle let alone cycle through the French countryside on her own.

Genevieve nodded as she read the names and addresses and traced the route between villages with her fingertip on the map.

'All set, Angelique?' Marcel asked.

She knew Yves was testing her and it was obvious Marcel and Henri knew that too because neither of them could look her in the eye.

'I'll get ready,' she said, going to the ladder.

'A bath's out of the question, I'm afraid,' Yves said sarcastically.

She ignored him and continued up the steps. Once at the top, she took off the flying overalls to reveal a blouse and skirt such as might be worn by a country girl. She put on espadrilles and combed her hair to remove any straw, then using the compact she'd been given by Vera Atkins before she left, she applied lipstick.

'As far as possible, don't ever look as though you've slept under a hedge — even if you have,' her instructors had told the trainees. 'Don't give the Germans an opportunity to think you're suspicious. And what looks more suspicious than a man or woman who's been sleeping rough?'

The men gaped as she descended the ladder.

'Very nice,' said Henri with a cheeky wink.

'You kept Marcel waiting while you put on lipstick?' Yves said with an angry frown.

She ignored him and, taking the handlebars, wheeled the bicycle outside, to find Marcel.

'Angelique! You might look lovely but haven't you forgotten something?' It was Yves and his tone was scathing.

She stopped peered over her shoulder, looking for whatever it was he thought she'd forgotten.

'These!' he said furiously, holding up the addresses and map between forefinger and thumb, 'You're going to need to look at these again or you'll be wandering all over the countryside not knowing where you're going.'

'I've memorised them,' Genevieve said sweetly and recited the four names and addresses as well, road by road, the route she would take.

Henri burst out laughing, 'She's not just a pretty face, old man!'

To Genevieve's surprise, Yves smiled at her and nodded his head in approval, 'Well, what are you waiting for? You'll need to get going if you want to be back by nightfall.'

She recognised his challenge. In all probability, he knew it was impossible to cycle that route in the time he'd allowed her but whatever it cost her, she'd do her best to be back before he expected.

★　★　★

Genevieve followed Marcel along the road. He wasn't cycling very fast — certainly not as fast as she could go — so she knew that once they got through the checkpoint, she'd have to go much faster if she wanted to be back at the barn before night. The clouds hung heavily over the countryside, and she wondered how long it would be before it began to rain.

Finally, they reached the checkpoint. The guards were searching a vegetable truck.

'The soldiers aren't usually this thorough,' Marcel whispered, 'I wonder if they know about last night's delivery from England? I'll have to let Yves know. We certainly don't want to bring arms through here.'

There were two vans and a car behind the vegetable truck, all waiting to be searched and Genevieve could see it was going to be a long time before she and Marcel got through.

She climbed off the bicycle and made a show of retying the ribbon of her espadrille, then looking at her watch and sadly shaking her head. One of the guards standing by watching the others remove boxes of vegetables from the truck, strolled towards her, his rifle over his shoulder.

'Everything all right, Mademoiselle?' he asked, not able to take his eyes off Genevieve's legs.

'I had a stone in my shoe, but it's all right now, thank you.' She extended her leg and rotated her ankle as if checking the ribbons were straight. The guard stared at her leg, mesmerised.

'Do you think it'll be much longer before I can go through? I'm so late already,' Genevieve asked looking at her watch then up at the soldier.

'Well, I suppose I could check your papers . . .'

'Would you? I'd be so grateful . . .'

She handed him her identity card and after a quick glance, he lifted the cover off her bicycle basket with the tip of his rifle and peered inside. There was an apple and a piece of cheese wrapped in cloth which Henri had given her.

With one last look at her legs, the soldier jerked his head at the check-point, 'Off you go, Mademoiselle,' he said.

'Oh, thank you so much!' Genevieve said, lowering her head and gazing up at him through her lashes, then without looking back at Marcel, she straddled the bicycle and rode off, as if she really was a young, lone French girl who was late.

She cycled slowly, aware that to race along would arouse suspicion but once around the bend and out of sight of any Germans, she pedalled furiously, trying to make up for lost time. The houses she needed to find were not on main roads and she bumped over rutted tracks, but with the map firmly fixed in her memory, she found each house and after using passwords to ensure she was passing on Yves' message to the correct people, she told them the arms were ready to be picked up and that it might be best to avoid the checkpoint she'd just passed through.

She got lost once but luckily, when she'd realised her mistake, she discovered that to get back on the correct road to the barn, she could freewheel down a hill and after hours of cycling, Genevieve arrived back well before sunset. She'd been drenched by a sudden downpour, her muscles ached, and she was saddle-sore but she gritted her teeth and walked as normally as possible into the barn. She wouldn't give Yves the satisfaction of seeing how much it hurt.

Henri and Yves were deep in conversation with two men who were packing Sten guns and grenades in a large crate, ready to spirit away to an arms cache. They turned in surprise when they heard her enter.

She recited the names of the men she'd visited and their addresses, then added, 'Messages delivered to all four.'

'Good show, my dear,' said Henri.

Yves merely nodded his head slightly to acknowledge her words, but she thought she detected the glimmer of a smile.

⋆ ⋆ ⋆

The following afternoon, Genevieve was relieved when the last of the guns and explosives were taken and the bales of straw re-stacked to the farmer's satisfaction. After a second night in the loft sleeping on straw, she was looking forward to having a bed. Yves had said as soon as the arms had gone, he'd take her to a safe house.

She spent the morning with Henri, poring over a map as she showed him the sites London wanted to be targeted. Yves had been too busy to sit with them as he'd been supervising the men who'd come to take away the guns and ammunition.

'So, Angelique,' Yves said as he joined Genevieve and Henri, 'What are our orders?'

Genevieve briefly ran through the list of targets and Henri summarised their thoughts and plans. Yves slowly nodded his approval, gazing into the distance as his mind buzzed with possible threats and hazards. For the first time, Genevieve had a chance to study his face without him knowing and was surprised to see how handsome he was despite the two-day old stubble and the unruly blonde hair which he had a habit of raking with his fingers when he was troubled.

Yves bit his bottom lip. 'It's all possible, although the tank factory's going to be a problem. We don't have any contacts working there.'

'Yet,' said Henri, 'we don't have contacts yet.'

'Can you think of anyone?' Yves asked, 'We'd need more information about the running of the plant and a better floor plan than this . . . ' He moved the aerial photograph and the diagrams Genevieve had brought from London closer and screwed up his eyes as he scanned the documents to glean the maximum information.

'This shows the external security points,' he said tapping various places on the photograph and gives us a good idea of the area but this . . . ' he put the plan on top. 'It doesn't give much detail of the interior. We can't plan a night-time raid if we don't know what we're up against.'

'I'm afraid it was the best SOE could do,' Genevieve said. 'Apparently one of the other circuits had a contact working in the factory and he gave us this much information but before he could pass our agent a complete drawing, he was caught and then the whole circuit was arrested.'

Henri rubbed his chin thoughtfully, 'I think I might know a chap who could help us. His brother used to work at the factory.'

'Why didn't you say?' Yves said.

'Because he's a slippery character and definitely not to be trusted. But if we pay him enough, we might buy his loyalty. The money Genevieve brought from London will certainly come in handy. If you like, I'll try to set up a meeting and we can sound him out.'

'In the meantime,' Yves said, 'I'll get Marcel to see what he can find out.'

'Right,' said Henri, checking his watch, 'I've got to get back to my room. I've a sched in an hour's time and need to get the wireless set up. It'll be heaven to sleep in a proper bed tonight.'

The farmer gave them a lift in his van and dropped them at the edge of town, accelerating away so prying eyes wouldn't see them all together. Henri set off in one direction with his precious wireless concealed in his suitcase and Yves and Genevieve in the opposite direction.

'It's not far,' said Yves, 'Dr Gaston and his wife live at the end of this road.' Then, as a truck containing German soldiers rounded the corner and came towards them, Yves put his arm around her shoulders and placing his other hand on her cheek, he turned her abruptly towards him and rested his forehead against hers.

'Act as if we are lovers!' he whispered.

Realising his action had shielded both their faces from the Germans, she played along, putting her arms around his waist, pulling him close. The truck passed by and she was sure it had gone but still, he held her and then, just as abruptly as he'd pulled her close, he let his arm fall from her shoulders.

'I'm sorry,' he said and for the first time since she'd met him, he appeared uncomfortable — and, she thought, even slightly embarrassed.

'I've had dealings with that German sergeant before and I thought it better for both of us if he didn't recognise me.' After that, Yves remained silent until they reached Dr Gaston's house at the end of the road.

Blanche Gaston, the doctor's wife, opened the door and, with a quick glance left and right, ushered them into her living room. As soon as Yves had introduced Genevieve, he slipped out of

128

the back of the house and was gone.

Genevieve was drawn to Blanche immediately. The older woman's warmth and strength of character were obvious and when she showed Genevieve a framed photograph of her son, Pierre, who'd been arrested by the Germans for taking part in a sabotage attempt, her eyes filled with tears. Blanche said he'd been sent to a concentration camp, and they'd had no news from him for several months so she and her husband would do whatever it took to undermine the German occupation.

Genevieve was tempted to tell Blanche about JP's disappearance but she hadn't spoken of it to anyone and somehow, it didn't seem right to burden her host with her own sadness.

Blanche led Genevieve upstairs to her bedroom and then showed her the doctor's surgery, waiting room and reception where Genevieve would be working. In fact, Blanche would do most of the office work allowing Genevieve to travel on her bicycle, delivering medicines and running errands for Dr Gaston. Her 'job', would cover the fact that she was actually carrying messages for Yves and the Tulip Circuit when necessary. Blanche told her that if Yves or Henri wanted to meet her, they would send a coded message. If someone should come into the surgery and tell her Uncle René had run out of his medicine, she would know she should go to the Café Fleur de Lys in the main square that day. Her response should be to ask when Uncle René had run out of his medicine. Whatever time she was told, would be when she needed to be at the rendezvous.

'Don't worry, Angelique,' said Blanche when she saw Genevieve's worried expression, 'it's a lot to take in but I'll be here and together, we'll get through it.'

Dr Gaston, who'd been out on a call, arrived shortly after and Genevieve took to him immediately, too. He was much smaller than his wife and had a rather disarming way of peering over his spectacles but his manner was gentle and she knew she was going to be safe in their house — at least, as safe as one could be in Occupied France.

★　★　★

Over the next few weeks, Genevieve got to know her hosts and some of the regular patients, as well as more of the resisters who worked with the Tulip Circuit. She ran errands for Dr Gaston and under the cover of her work for him, she also passed messages to and from Yves and Henri.

She carried bottles of medicine and tablets in her bicycle basket and since she passed so frequently through the various checkpoints, the German guards usually waved her through and if they stopped her to look in the basket, they didn't bother to search thoroughly.

Yves' initial hostility subsided to a grudging approval as she showed herself to be punctual, reliable and resourceful. However, he remained aloof and had as little to do with her as possible . . . until one day when she was

131

summoned to the Café Fleur de Lys. Henri met her and instructed her to go to the Escoffier's farmhouse that evening because they'd received information a German consignment of arms was arriving by train the following night. Genevieve slipped away after dinner and cycled to the remote farmhouse where she met Yves, Henri and several members of the local Resistance.

There was bad news. Marcel had narrowly missed being arrested by a German patrol while sabotaging a telephone exchange the previous evening and, as he'd escaped, he'd been shot. Luckily, the bullet had only grazed his leg but he'd also twisted his ankle and it would be a few weeks before he'd be able to take part in any of the operations Yves had planned.

'Shall we call it off?' one of the resisters asked Yves. 'We've lost three men this month and with Marcel out of action — '

'I'll go,' Genevieve interrupted.

The men looked at her as if she'd suggested she'd sprout wings and fly.

'No,' Yves said quickly, 'it's too risky.'

'This is what I trained for!' Genevieve said.

She stood up and grabbed one of the Sten guns, quickly disassembling it. The men's eyes didn't leave her fingers as she then re-assembled it and placed it on the table. They seemed startled but impressed at her speed and dexterity.

'I have experience with plastic explosives and know the best place to blow up a train, depending on if you want to cause disruption to services or damage the train and its passengers . . . ' she added, 'So, will you take me?'

'If we're going to do this,' Henri said, 'we're going to need help. I say yes.' The other men around the table nodded their approval.

Only Yves remained silent. Finally, he nodded too. 'If that's what you all want . . . '

'We don't have a choice,' said Henri.

'Our lady with the code name Heart, is showing hers to be fearless.'

★　★　★

That night, Genevieve barely slept, worried she'd somehow let the men down. She'd shown off her proficiency with guns and displayed her bravery in demanding to go, but would her courage fail her once she was actually there? It was all very well having trained but quite another to face the enemy in their own territory.

She wished she hadn't chosen the SOE code name Heart. It wasn't the sloppy, sentimental image she wanted to portray and only Henri, so far, had used it in a positive way when he'd suggested her heart was fearless.

Well, it was too late to back out now. They'd planned where to blow up the rails and ambush the train and had informed many of the resisters to be there, ready to seize whatever they could carry before escaping into the darkness.

'It's a shame it's happening tonight,' Henri said frowning at the black clouds which were already rolling towards them. 'There's going to be a terrific storm. It'll be slippery and dark. Not easy going at all.'

However, the opportunity of causing such havoc to the Germans and of acquiring so many weapons was too great to miss.

'You know, I think the storm might work in our favour,' said Yves, thoughtfully.

Indeed, it appeared he was right and that, despite seeming otherwise, fate was actually with them.

The lashing rain put the Germans off guard.

Firstly, who would have thought the resisters would be out in such numbers on so dreadful a night? Secondly, it reduced visibility, making the soldiers less diligent. Even more importantly, the storm with its booming peals of thunder and brilliant flashes of lightning that streaked across the sky, masked the mighty roar of the explosion which blew up the rails and sent the train hurtling down a steep embankment.

As soon as the carriages came to a standstill, French resisters poured out of their hiding places and grabbed whatever weapons they could carry while others dealt with the German soldiers.

It all happened with shocking rapidity.

On a still, calm night, the explosion and crash would've been heard for miles around, prompting soldiers to pour out of the nearby garrison and be at the site within minutes, but with the deafening thunder overhead, there was a delay before news of the sabotage reached the German officers. By the time the soldiers arrived on the scene, the rain had turned the area into a slippery, treacherous slope, hindering their trucks from getting to the overturned carriages and wagons.

It had been a thoroughly profitable

night's work and miraculously, there had been no casualties among the saboteurs.

Genevieve met Henri in the Café Fleur de Lys the following afternoon and he congratulated her on her part in the action. 'By the way, Angelique, I thought you ought to know I reported our success to London. They're very pleased. Oh, and when you arrived here, Yves asked me to request London send a male agent to replace you.'

Genevieve felt as if she'd been punched in the stomach.

'London have let me know they've someone trained, ready to come out.'

She nodded and swallowed her tears. So much for proving herself last night!

'I told Yves this morning,' Henri continued, 'and he said to tell London he no longer needs a replacement and that he's happy to have you as part of the circuit.'

'Really?' Genevieve was thrilled.

'But if you want to go, I'll let London know.'

'No! Of course, I don't want to go!'

'Then be at the Escoffier's farm at eighteen hundred hours. Yves has called a meeting.'

★ ★ ★

Genevieve arrived at the farm early and was welcomed by Madame Escoffier, who escorted her into the kitchen with its long, wooden table.

Yves was the only person there and he looked up and nodded curtly. 'Good work, last night, Angelique,' he said and glanced back at the map and diagrams in front of him on the table.

Praise indeed from a man who rarely showed any emotion, Genevieve thought. He pulled out the chair next to him to indicate she should sit, then slid one of the diagrams in front of her.

'We'll wait until Henri gets here but this is our next target,' he said moving the diagram so they could both see it.

It felt good to be included for once.

'Henri told me you were offered a

replacement for me . . . ' she said.

'Hmm.' Yves didn't look up.

'Well, I just wanted to thank you.'

'We're too busy at the moment to break a new courier in,' he said and she suppressed a smile at his explanation. That wasn't what Henri had said he'd told London.

He changed the subject and started pointing out potential difficulties in the surrounding areas of a telephone exchange that would be their next target. Genevieve took the opportunity to glance up from where his finger was indicating on the map, to his face. Their heads were inches apart and she could see the sprinkling of freckles over the bridge of his nose. There was a strange warm glow in the pit of her stomach and she fought to keep her attention on the map rather than his face, but the memory of him putting his arms around her and holding her tightly kept breaking her concentration. His hand had held her face to his and in her imagination, she could still feel his cheek pressed to hers. There was the faintest hint of sandalwood which she'd detected on the few occasions she'd been as close to him as she was now. Closing her eyes, she breathed in the heady scent she'd come to associate with him.

'Angelique? Am I boring you?'

'No! Of course not. I was just . . . um . . . memorising the map,' she said knowing she hadn't been taking notice at all.

Henri rushed in, a smear of mud across his chin and on his clothes. 'Lordy, lordy! I thought the game was up!' he said, placing his suitcase on the table and sinking into a chair.

'What happened?' Yves stood up so abruptly, his chair fell over backwards.

'I was just in the middle of my sched to London and the signal must've been picked up by a Jerry RDF van. I noticed a butcher's van parked up the road when I met Angelique earlier. I should've come here earlier and sent my messages, but it's always easy to be

140

wise after the event.'

Genevieve knew German RDF or Radio Direction Finding vans travelled around towns and cities searching for radio signals, often disguised as company vans such as a butcher's van. It was forbidden to have a radio, so if a signal was detected, the Germans knew they'd located someone communicating with their enemies.

'How did you get away?' Yves asked.

'Out the window. I rented that room because the next-door roof was easily accessible. Just a short drop and away. I won't be able to go back now, though. The Gestapo'll be watching it from now on. At least I was faster than the soldiers!'

Henri was laughing as he told them but she could see his hands were trembling. SOE radio operators had the shortest life expectancy of all the operatives because if they were found with a forbidden radio, there was no possibility of explaining its presence.

'And the other bad news,' Henri

added, 'is the town is crawling with soldiers. I think our little effort last night must have stirred up a hornet's nest. I ran into one of our Resistance chaps on my way home from seeing Angelique and he said he'd heard an important Jerry officer was about to visit the garrison. After last night's entertainment, they're going to make an enormous effort to prove they're efficient. My friend mentioned house-to-house searches.'

Yves sighed. 'I think we might need to lie low for a while. Perhaps even move out of the district at least until things quieten down. With Marcel out of action, it's harder to make new contacts.'

'I agree. D'you want to leave immediately?'

'No, the last thing we need is to risk being out after curfew. Stay the night here, Henri, then tomorrow morning, we'll keep a low profile.'

'There's a safe house in Chinon,' Henri said, 'As soon as I get there I'll let London know things are going to be quiet for a few days.' Henri went upstairs to hide his wireless set.

'Will you stay here, Yves?' Genevieve asked.

'I don't know. I wouldn't want to bring trouble to Mr Escoffier and his wife. How about you?'

'I don't suppose they'll be looking for a girl, so I'll probably stay with Dr Gaston.'

Yves bit his bottom lip, deep in thought. 'If they're going to carry out house-to-house searches . . . ' he didn't finish the sentence.

'I know somewhere,' said Genevieve. 'My grandfather owns a château and vineyards near Saumur. It's quite a large estate in the middle of the country and I know he'd let us stay.'

What are you doing? D'you really want to spend more time with this man who a short while ago thought so much of you he wanted London to replace you? Strangely, the answer was yes. Yes, indeed, she did want to get to know

Yves better — and to make him accept her fully.

To Genevieve's surprise, Yves readily agreed and arranged to meet her the following morning at Dr Gaston's house.

They planned to cycle, mostly along the banks of the Loire, keeping away from busy roads and roadblocks, as far from German eyes as possible. She would enter the estate covertly and make her way to her grandfather's study on the ground floor. When he was alone, she'd tap on the window to attract his attention and explain why she was there. Grand-père had many members of staff and not having visited him for some time, she had no idea if they would betray her presence.

★   ★   ★

They arrived at Château Saint Pierre in the late afternoon and Genevieve suggested they hide in the cave where

144

she'd once played with her brother, then wait until nightfall before she attempted to contact her grandfather. The cave had once been used to store wine because it maintained a constant temperature all year round but it had obviously not been visited for some time and it took her a while to find the opening among the undergrowth.

From their elevated position, they could see the rows of vines like stripes across the countryside and they shared some bread and cheese they'd bought in a village earlier.

Yves was relaxed and asked her about her life in France. 'Did you want to be an SOE operative in France because of your family here?' he asked.

'Partly. I love France, and I love England. I belong in both and it breaks my heart to see how the Nazis are tearing this country apart. Given the opportunity they'll do the same to England. But . . . ' She paused, 'I'm also here because of my brother, JP.' It was painful and personal, but perhaps it was being in the place where they'd both played as children or perhaps she wanted to confide in Yves, who, being a fellow SOE agent, would surely understand.

'Where is he?'

'I don't know. He was sent out to France by the SOE months ago but nothing's been heard of him for some time.'

'I'm sorry, Angelique . . . will you look for him?'

Genevieve shook her head sadly, 'I've no idea where to start. But the stupid thing is, every time I see a queue of people waiting to get through a checkpoint or I go into the market, I scan everyone's faces. I know the chances of finding him are negligible but at least if I'm in the same country, I feel closer.'

She told him about her two homes and for the first time, he told her about having spent his childhood in France when his father worked in the British Embassy. When he retired, the family

146

moved to Dorset and Yves had joined the Army.

'By the way,' she said, 'I know secrecy's vital and agents shouldn't tell each other their real names but if you're going to meet my grandfather, he's not going to call me by my field name, Angelique. My real name is Genevieve.'

He repeated her name slowly, as if savouring it.

'Yes,' he said, nodding his head slowly, 'that suits you. It's a beautiful name.'

Genevieve blushed. 'May I know yours?'

'Captain Mark Leyton,' he said formally. 'Pleased to make your acquaintance, Miss . . . ?'

'Lawrence. Genevieve Lawrence.'

He was a different man to the one she'd met when she'd been dropped into France so many weeks ago. High above the vineyards, it was as if they were inhabiting their own private world in which the Germans and the war had no part.

As the sun dipped below the horizon, they hid their bicycles and set off, bending double as they ran between the rows of vines. There were several cars parked in front of the château and a hubbub of voices came from inside.

'It sounds like your grandfather's entertaining,' Yves said with a frown, 'You'll have to wait until everyone's gone before you contact him.'

'That's strange, Grand-père doesn't like lots of people for dinner.'

'Get down!' Yves said, 'That car's German.' They crouched down and peered through the tangle of vine leaves. 'All the cars are German. It looks as though he's got quite a party in there.'

'I hope you're not suggesting my grand-père's a collaborator!'

'No, of course not, it's more likely they've requisitioned the château.' Yves whispered as she crept closer to the house, 'You can't help.'

The sound of dogs barking stopped

her progress and she crawled back towards Yves.

A door burst open and a portly German officer strode out into the courtyard. 'Vannier! Shut those dogs up before I shoot them!' He struck out at an elderly man who hurried past him, catching him on the side of the head. The grey-haired man staggered, then recovering his balance, he limped as fast as he could towards where the dogs were tethered and spoke to them soothingly in French.

'Grand-père!'

Yves put a restraining hand on her arm and shook his head.

'You'll only make things worse for him if you're caught. Come,' he said, drawing her gently away.

'What're we going to do now?' Genevieve asked when they got back to the cave.

'We'll have to sleep here tonight. We don't want to be caught out after curfew — that's taking a needless risk — and then tomorrow, we'll make our way back. There are a few safe houses we can try on the way. Henri thought the fuss in the garrison would die down within a day or two. I don't suppose the visiting officers will stay long.'

Covering themselves with the spare clothes they'd brought, they lay close, keeping each other warm. The scent of sandalwood filled her nostrils and roused her senses making it hard to sleep.

Their trip to Château Saint Pierre had been a wasted journey. She'd promised Yves a bed but instead, they were lying on the floor of a cave. Even worse, she'd seen her grandfather — much thinner than she'd ever seen him and obviously in pain — and it appeared he was being forced to host German officers in his home.

Yet, lying next to Yves, a wave of happiness washed over her. She could see his face as clearly in her mind's eye as if she were actually looking at him. Every feature was etched in her memory — grey eyes with long lashes, lips that made her catch her breath when he smiled, blonde hair with the fringe that flopped over his forehead.

She tried to remember Eric's face but it was as faint as a watercolour painting that had been left out in the rain. Even Sonny's face was indistinct.

Could she be falling for Yves?

3

The barest suggestion of movement near Yves' face woke him in an instant. He sat up, his pistol in hand, peering into the utter blackness. Since he'd been in France working for SOE, he spent his nights semi-alert, ready to escape.

It was too dark to see, but the scurrying sounds and the scuffling of tiny stones over the surface of the cave told him he'd been brought to a state of complete alertness by an animal. The beam of his torch soon caught the culprit — a lizard. It had probably detected the heat of his and Angelique's bodies and wanted to warm itself.

Yves gently breathed out, tension draining from his body, turned the torch off and quietly put the gun down. Angelique had stirred but not woken, he realised sadly. Had the lizard been something more sinister, she'd have had no idea until it was too late. She still had so much to learn about staying alive in an occupied country and he dreaded the thought she might not live long enough to learn it. But perhaps he was being unfair, after all, a man — even a stealthy man — would make more noise than a lizard.

Yves gently settled down again, not wanting to waken Angelique. He smiled as she sighed in her sleep and moved closer to him, probably seeking his warmth — just as the lizard had done.

He remembered that first shocking moment he'd seen her when Marcel had brought her from the adjacent field after she'd jumped from the aircraft. He simply hadn't been able to believe London had sent a girl to be the circuit's new courier but there she was, dressed in a flying suit with her parachute bundled up in Marcel's arms.

Yves had been furious, with Marcel for defying him, and with London, but most of all with Angelique for being a girl — and such a beautiful one at that. She was the sort of girl a man wanted to protect and he'd seen how the others had been distracted from the vital work of hiding the weapons which had accompanied her on her journey across the Channel.

He'd noticed his men's eyes follow Angelique with inquisitive and admiring glances, although to her credit she'd seemed unaware of the attention. If she'd known, she'd done a good job of ignoring them and certainly couldn't be accused of provoking such a reaction. Even the usually steady Henri was smitten with Angelique, teasingly calling her his Fearless Heart. Yves had to work hard to maintain the discipline he hadn't needed to think about before she'd arrived.

It wasn't as if she was unaware of the effect she had on men because she put it to good use dazzling guards at road blocks, getting through with the minimum of searching or intervention. It seemed the Germans assumed their enemies came in the shape of strong men. That a beautiful, fragile girl like Angelique might be a threat didn't occur to them — or at least it hadn't so far. She'd shown herself to be resourceful and, as Henri had described her, fearless. The memory of her losing her temper and seizing that automatic weapon, stripping it down and reassembling it faster than any of his men could have done made him smile.

For the first time, Yves conceded that perhaps London had made a shrewd decision in training women operatives and dropping them behind enemy lines. They could be as effective as men, sometimes even more so.

Yet for Yves, she was simply more to worry about. He was concerned about the men in his circuit and people like the Gastons and the Escoffiers and countless others who opened their homes to British agents and French resisters, offering to shelter them, often at extreme risk to themselves. But

Angelique? He had to admit, she troubled him most of all. Or perhaps more accurately, it was his reaction to her which troubled him most of all. It was many months since a girl had been on his mind . . .

When his father retired and moved back to England from France, Yves had joined the Army. At a ball, he'd met Lydia and fallen deeply in love — or so he'd thought. Every waking moment he wasn't with her was spent remembering the last time they'd been together or anticipating the next time he'd see her. Like Angelique. Lydia was beautiful although as blonde as Angelique was dark. Both girls appeared to be unaware of the spell they cast over men, but in the case of Lydia, it had all been an act. He discovered too late that she knew exactly what she was doing in playing one man off against another.

As for Angelique . . . Yves wasn't experienced enough with women to know if she was simply more cunning than Lydia. However, since he had no intention of becoming romantically involved with Angelique, it was irrelevant.

Lydia had strung him along, led him to believe they'd spend the rest of their lives together. He'd made plans, working out how far a captain's salary would stretch, explaining their standard of living would improve as he was promoted. At first, she brushed all thoughts of denying herself anything away, saying her papa would ensure she had what she wanted. When he told her he wouldn't accept anything from her father, she became petulant and they'd argued. He'd been distraught but his pride wouldn't allow him to accept money from her father, even on her behalf and he'd stayed away, sure she'd give in and see reason.

Too late, he realised Lydia never gave in and did not let reason stand in the way of what she wanted. She'd settled on a wealthy farmer instead and soon after, announced her engagement.

Yves' father bought a large estate in

Dorset and Lydia discovered that although she'd thought Yves a simple army captain, he was heir to a fortune and one day would be far richer than her new fiancé. She told him she'd made a dreadful mistake and she really loved him. Her father had forced her hand, she said, but now she realised she couldn't live without him and was willing to defy her father to be with him.

Yves wanted to believe her but something — perhaps pride, perhaps common sense — stopped him and gradually, the love he'd felt for Lydia turned into pity, and then disdain.

Love? It was meaningless. It'd merely been trickery on Lydia's part and self-delusion on his.

No, Yves would never give his heart to anyone again. In time, he might get over Lydia and consider love again but right now it was the last thing on his mind. His chances of surviving this war, however long it took to run its course, were slim. Time was limited and he had to concentrate on his job.

* * *

After their night in the cave, Yves spent two days with Angelique in a safe house where he contacted other Resistance groups who might be able to assist the Tulip Circuit. Angelique insisted on coming with him and, he had to admit, when they walked through the streets, her presence seemed to offer him a cloak of invisibility because a strange man might easily be marked out as suspicious, but a young couple walking hand in hand, each with eyes only for the other? No one would suspect the two sweethearts were really British agents on their way to a meeting with members of the French Resistance.

He marvelled at his acting skills. He was playing the role of Angelique's lover so convincingly he had to remind himself the intimacy must stop when they were alone. On the first day, it had been so pleasurable sitting in a café, holding hands and staring into each other's eyes that he'd deliberately prolonged their time together.

They'd arranged to meet a new contact in the café but when they'd arrived, Yves was dismayed to see lots of German officers at the tables. It was too late to change the arrangements. When the Frenchman entered, Yves and Angelique feigned delight at meeting an old friend by chance and greeted each other with kisses on both cheeks.

Over coffee, they passed him the necessary information, saying it had been too long since they'd got together and that he was sure they'd be seeing each other again very soon. Yves knew this meant he and his men were happy to work with Tulip Circuit and they'd be in contact via the couriers who passed messages between groups.

Yves and Angelique should have left the café then, but he'd ordered more coffee. It wasn't bad quality, he told himself, and that was probably why it had more than its fair share of German customers. Yet deep down he knew it was more to do with the fact that, for as long as it took to sip the drink, he could hold Angelique's hands and look into her violet, almond-shaped eyes, pretending they were a couple.

He told her about his childhood in France, his schools, his friends and his younger brother. She in turn told him about life on her grandfather's estate in the Loire. They didn't speak of surnames or towns and if any of the Germans had been listening in, they couldn't possibly have gleaned any information which would have incriminated either him or Angelique. They were simply two young people who'd grown up in different parts of France sharing their lives. But then, Yves began to regret his earlier impulsiveness . . .

'Look at the lovers!' one of the German officers said to another in heavily accented French — obviously for their benefit.

'Lucky man,' another of them said, 'I hope he looks after his girl well or I'll be on her tail!'

'Well, you may not have long to wait,

we're recruiting strong, young men to work for the Reich. Men just like him. So, wait long enough, Heinz and she could be yours!'

Their voices were slurred. Yves knew they'd been drinking heavily and was furious with himself for putting Angelique in danger. With seeming indifference, Yves signalled to the waiter for the bill and left as soon as he could without making eye contact with the officers.

Two women entered the café as Yves was paying and the officers' attention immediately switched to them, asking if they wanted to join them. One appeared to want nothing to do with them but the other was tempted by a glass of cognac. As one of the officers increased his offer to include dinner, Yves and Angelique calmly left.

Yves was quiet on the way home, ashamed of himself for risking Angelique. It was unlikely the officers would have done anything although he knew they thought themselves above the law and if they set their mind to something, they could do as they liked. What might an unscrupulous man do to get an attractive woman alone with him? Yves felt a shadow pass over him. He must never do anything so foolish again.

* * *

The following day, word arrived from Henri that things had settled down and it was safe to return. Marcel's leg had healed, although he now walked with a slight limp, but he greeted Yves warmly when they met at the Escoffier farm.

'There's something I'd like to ask you before the others come, Marcel,' Yves said. 'Can you make some enquiries for me about an SOE agent who went missing some time last year?'

'One of yours?'

'No, this man was with the Jonquille Circuit near Paris. A collaborator infiltrated the group and most of the agents disappeared.'

'Yes, I remember. It was shocking.

Well, I can try to find out if anyone has any idea what happened. What's the man called?'

'His SOE name is Minotaur. The other members of his circuit would have known him as Benoit and his official papers showed him as Sébastien Mossé. His real name is Jean-Paul Lawrence.'

'Why are you so interested in this man? D'you think he was the one who betrayed Jonquille?'

'Absolutely not. I'm asking for Angelique but I don't want you to tell her. It's unlikely we'll find anything and I don't want to build her hopes up.'

'Ah! Angelique. This man is important to her?'

Yves nodded. 'Her brother.'

'Ah! Not the man who gave her the tiny heart on her watch, then?'

'I don't know.' Yves hadn't noticed the heart.

'Obviously not! A heart isn't the kind of gift one makes to a sister.'

'I've no idea,' Yves said, not wanting

to think about who'd given her such a gift.

'Is Angelique married?' Marcel persisted.

'I don't know. We've never discussed her marital status,' Yves said, not wanting to talk about the possibility she had someone special.

'I'd be very surprised if she wasn't. She's a fine-looking woman,' Marcel said.

'It makes no difference to me,' said Yves sharply, 'so long as she does her job while she's here, that's all that matters.'

'So why the interest in Angelique's brother?'

'She was very close to him and at least she'd know one way or the other if he was still alive.'

'I'll do what I can, mon ami.'

★ ★ ★

Genevieve returned home to a warm greeting from Blanche and her husband, and the following day she resumed her bicycle deliveries and filing in Dr Gaston's office. His patients had become accustomed to seeing her in the office or on her bicycle, and she was touched that several said they'd been worried by her absence, so she told them she'd been visiting her sick grandfather.

Several days later, Marcel limped into the doctor's surgery and asked Genevieve for a prescription for more ointment.

'Here's the name of what I had before,' he said passing a small slip of paper to Genevieve.

'I'll check with Dr Gaston,' she said, taking the paper with her. Once outside the waiting room, she read the message which told her to be at the Escoffier's farm that evening.

'Dr Gaston will see you get the ointment,' Genevieve said when she went back in the waiting room. He nodded and left.

⋆　⋆　⋆

When she arrived at the farm, Henri, Yves and Marcel were already at the table, staring at a wireless set, their faces strained.

'We're waiting for the BBC Personal Messages,' Henri explained. 'If we hear 'Pierre has pulled a rabbit from his hat' we know there'll be a parachute drop tonight. We're going to blow up the tank manufacturing plant and Yves requested guns and explosives days ago, but the weather's been so bad the planes haven't been able to get here. Tonight, though, we think the consignment will arrive.'

Each evening after the news, the BBC's French Service broadcast a list of seemingly meaningless phrases which were actually codes intended for resistance groups and circuits across France.

'Before we begin, please listen to some personal messages . . . ' the BBC presenter on the wireless said. 'I'm going to cut my hair . . . The fire went out yesterday . . . Please buy some

bread on your way home tonight
. . . My umbrella is green, yours is blue
. . . Pierre has pulled a rabbit from his
hat . . . Let's go to Paris on the
train . . . '

Yves switched the wireless set off, his
face triumphant. They didn't need to
hear anymore. The code told them the
drop would happen at midnight in the
field where Genevieve had landed
several months before, and the earlier
tension in the farm kitchen evaporated,
giving way to smiles.

Yves spread the aerial photographs of
the tank factory over the long table and
Marcel took papers from his inside
pocket and unfolded them.

'Jacques, the foreman at the factory,
is a member of the Resistance. He's
drawn these plans of the interior of the
factory and suggested the best locations
to destroy so we cause maximum
disruption to productivity,' Marcel said
sliding the sheets across the table to
Yves.

'He says it'll take two men to set the

explosives and he proposes to smuggle them in after the workers have gone home and the factory closes for the day. He'll hide them in a cupboard and then on his way out, he'll leave the side gate furthest from the German sentries unlocked. After that, it's up to the two men inside to blow the place to bits.'

Yves nodded, 'Excellent. Henri and I will go — '

'That doesn't make sense,' Genevieve cut in, 'It should be you and me, Yves. Henri is too important as the wireless operator to risk on a job like this. If something happens to him, we lose contact with London and that means no more weapons or assistance.'

'Absolutely not!' said Yves.

'Angelique has a point,' Marcel said. 'This is going to be risky. I'm sorry to have to say this Henri, mon ami, but you aren't as slim or as nimble as Angelique, she'll be able to get into smaller places than you.'

'No, I don't like it,' Yves said but Genevieve could tell he was considering taking her rather than Henri. Marcel had been right and Yves was a shrewd leader; he knew what was sensible.

'Didn't you say to me only a few days ago that you were only interested in people doing their jobs?' Marcel asked.

Yves flushed, not admitting he'd said that about Angelique when Marcel had mentioned she might have a man at home.

'Is this what you want' Yves asked with a sigh.

'Yes, definitely.'

★　★　★

That evening, they waited at the dropping zone and as the aircraft passed overhead, box after box was pushed out. Each parachute opened and the crates floated through the night sky to eager, waiting hands. As Henri helped Yves carry one of the precious packages, his foot caught in a rabbit hole and he fell awkwardly, wrenching his knee.

Once the weapons were hidden, Dr

Gaston checked Henri's knee and advised him to avoid walking for a day or two. Genevieve would have to go with Yves to blow up the factory, whether he liked it or not.

She let herself into the Gaston's house and quietly climbed the stairs to her room. It was late and the crates had been heavy, so it had taken several hours to recover them from the dropping zone and hide them in the barn. She was tired but her mind was buzzing. Yves obviously wasn't happy about taking her into the factory but after Henri's accident earlier, she was the only choice.

Yves was an enigma. She knew the pretence of being a couple in public was to keep them safe but she'd enjoyed those times more than she cared to admit. As they'd left the barn, they'd been alone for a few minutes. To her surprise and delight, he'd caught hold of her hand.

'That's very pretty,' he'd said, indicating the heart charm which was attached to her watch bracelet. 'Did someone special give you that?'

The question had been so unexpected and surprising that, for a second, she hadn't known how to answer. After all, Sonny had been someone special to her — once.

He let her hand go and then said, 'It's none of my business. I just wondered.'

'It was just a friend,' she said but he'd already turned and she wasn't sure he'd heard.

It seemed pointless to chase after him to tell him it was simply a good luck charm. After all, he'd made it very clear he wasn't really interested.

* * *

As promised, Jacques the foreman was waiting by one of the rear gates to the factory. He looked about nervously and ushered Yves and Genevieve inside, quickly closing the gate and leading them across a delivery yard to the

172

factory. He slipped inside the building, checked the corridor, and beckoned for Yves and Genevieve to follow, then led them to a stationery cupboard.

'I've told the cleaners to go early, so stay quiet until they leave. The gate you came in by will be unlocked. Good luck.' He closed the door and hurried away, keen to be off the premises as quickly as possible.

* * *

Further along the corridor, unseen by Jacques, one of the machine operators was hiding in a doorway. He'd waited in the lavatories until everyone had gone home and then he'd planned to use some of the tools he'd taken from the workshop to break into the office. By chance, the previous day, he'd discovered the combination for the safe and after borrowing the key, he'd made a copy and returned the original.

Once he'd opened the safe, he intended to take all the money for the week's wages and escape. He'd arranged to slip across the demarcation line between Occupied France and the Free Zone to the south and then out of France. It depended on how much money he managed to steal as to his final destination but Spain would be the first stop. It had been a shock to see Jacques and two others still in the factory. If they didn't go soon, the cleaners would arrive and find him hiding in the lavatory.

He waited until all was quiet and then, as he was about to creep out, he heard the clanking of buckets. He cursed under his breath, his heart beating wildly with fear. How could he explain his presence if he was caught?

Opening the door a crack, he saw two cleaners, a man and a woman, with buckets and mops walking in the opposite direction. He knew they always cleaned the lavatories first, starting at the other end of the factory and working their way to where he was hiding. Then he had an idea. He'd get the money out of the safe immediately, hide on the factory floor, keeping out of the cleaners' way and then when he saw them go, he'd wait a few minutes and let himself out.

It was his only chance unless he simply left without the cash. But he needed that money for a new start and to pay off the debt he'd already incurred, paying in advance for his passage across the demarcation line.

He looked up and down the corridor. It was empty. He crept towards the office and the safe.

He vowed he'd never, ever do anything like this again. His fingers were shaking so much he could hardly rotate the dial to the correct numbers and sweat was dripping into his eyes, making him blink rapidly.

Finally, the door swung open and he saw the wage packets already made up for the following day. He scooped out all the envelopes into his bag, closed the safe door, locked it and spun the dial. Now when the cleaners came into the office, they wouldn't notice anything amiss. Hugging the bag to his chest, he hurried to the factory floor and crouched behind one of the presses.

He began to wish he'd chosen a hiding place with more leg room because his muscles were beginning to cramp but he dared not move now. Since he'd first seen the cleaners, he hadn't heard anything of them and he started to wonder if they had in fact gone home, when he was aware of a door opening into the workshop. Earlier, the cleaners had been talking loudly and rattling their buckets but now, if he hadn't been listening intently, he wouldn't have known they were there.

His breath was coming in ragged gasps and he pressed his hand to his chest, afraid the stressful situation would provoke a heart attack. How ironic it would be to have put himself through so much, and then tomorrow morning, be found dead behind the metal press with all the wage packets for the factory!

Two figures dressed in black — a man and a boy, or perhaps a woman — crept stealthily past him. It was as much as he could do to stop himself gasping. They weren't the cleaners, that was for sure. From his hiding place, he couldn't see where they'd gone but he could hear them.

Then the two mysterious figures moved further along to the machinery at the end of the factory.

He thought he heard the man say, 'Let's go!' And then they'd quickly but quietly left the factory floor through the door they'd entered.

He waited a few moments, straining to hear if they'd really gone. Presumably they, like he, were there to steal and he wondered what they'd got away with. His legs were numb when he finally crawled out of his hiding place and stood up unsteadily, listening intently in case the two figures returned, but he could hear nothing.

On a whim, he went over to the place he thought the two people had been. A sudden terrible thought struck him — perhaps they weren't thieves like him, perhaps they were saboteurs! And if so, what had they been doing?

Then he saw the plastic explosives.

For a second, his legs refused to respond to his brain's orders — *Run! Run! Run!*

He remained as if rooted to the spot. A rat ran across the floor in front of him, bringing him to his senses and he turned and fled, holding the bag of money to his chest as tightly as he could.

He had no thought now for cleaners, the two shadowy figures, or indeed the Germans — he simply wanted to get out of the building he knew was about to explode and he ran out of the factory into the delivery yard . . . straight into two soldiers.

★ ★ ★

Yves tapped his watch and pointed to the way out. They'd set the explosives and now had six minutes to clear the building and get to Marcel's van waiting down the street with its engine running ready to speed them away.

Genevieve nodded and followed him back to the door where Jacques had let them in. The large machines, pipes and equipment cast deep shadows in the factory turning it into a mysterious and menacing place — now even more threatening with the impending explosion which would hopefully destroy the entire site and significantly interrupt the production of German tanks.

Ahead of her, Yves cautiously opened the door to the delivery yard and motioning for her to slip through, he followed her and closed it behind him.

Genevieve grabbed his arm and drew him behind a large bin, her eyes wide with alarm. She'd spotted two soldiers turn the corner into the yard, deep in conversation.

Yves returned her look of horror. The yard was too wide for them to be able to run for it. The soldiers would have shot them before they reached the gate. He checked his watch — five minutes until detonation.

There was nothing they could do but wait. To run would be certain death.

The two guards strolled slowly through the yard, stopping to light cigarettes behind cupped hands and inhale deeply. A cat wandered by and one of them crouched down and stroked its chin but with its tail up and back arched, it slunk away, not interested in the soldier.

Four minutes to detonation.

The door Yves had carefully closed burst open and a man ran out clutching a large bundle to his chest. He didn't stop to close the door, but ran headlong into the startled guards.

'Halt!' one of them yelled, his rifle instantly at the ready. He fired at the fleeing figure, who dropped the bundle he'd been clutching and crumpled to the floor, screaming in agony.

One of the soldiers pulled him to his feet while the other stooped to pick up a bag, the contents spilling out over the cobblestones.

'What have we here?' he asked the man who was struggling to free his arm from the vice-like grip of the other soldier.

'It's going to blow up!' the man yelled, 'Get away from here!'

The two guards exchanged glances and one of them said, 'A likely story! You'd better come with us and explain why you have the wage packets for the entire factory in your bag.'

'You don't understand,' the man said, wrenching his arm free, 'the factory is going to — '

One of the soldiers slammed his rifle butt into the man's temple and his knees buckled. They dragged his unconscious body across the cobbles in the direction they'd come.

Seconds later, two shadowy figures crossed the delivery yard and slipped through the gate out into the street, where they ran as quickly as they could towards a waiting van and threw themselves in. It sped away just as a tremendous roar shook the factory. Further explosions rocked the area, windows shattered, throwing glass to the wind, girders grated against girders and sirens blared as the van raced towards town.

'You cut that fine!' Marcel growled, hunched over the steering wheel, a Gauloises cigarette clamped between his lips.

'Didn't we just!' Yves said, smiling at Genevieve.

* * *

Marcel braked sharply and Genevieve jumped from the van. Without turning back, she slipped into the rear entrance of the Gaston's garden, keeping to the shadows, and made her way to the back of the house, letting herself in. Locking the door behind her, she crept upstairs to bed.

Above the thumping of her heart she could hear sirens and the roar and crackle of an enormous fire some way off. Undressing quickly and climbing into bed, she lay there, eyes wide open and adrenaline still pumping through her body as she relived the moments when they'd heard the man tell the soldiers the factory was about to explode. Yves had held up one finger to warn her there was only one minute until the explosion would take place. She'd seen his brows draw together in hopelessness as if he was apologising to her. Then the soldiers had dragged the unconscious man away, giving them the chance to run.

Would Marcel and Yves manage to escape? The entire area would be crawling with police and soldiers searching for the saboteurs. 'Please, please,' she prayed, 'Please keep them safe.'

Sleep was not going to come that night. She was too wide awake. About thirty minutes after she'd arrived home, there was a hammering on the door. Genevieve got up and ruffled her hair to make it look as if she'd just awoken from a deep sleep. She listened from the landing to the conversation below.

'I assure you, officer, my wife and I have been in bed since ten.'

'We have a report of a van stopping near your property shortly after the explosion. Has anyone come to you for treatment?'

'No. I've been in bed with my wife for hours.'

'But I believe you have someone living in this house with you and your wife. Where is she?'

'Here I am,' said Genevieve, starting down the stairs. She spoke in the sleepiest voice she could manage and yawned. Dr Gaston turned to her and she could see the relief in his eyes. He obviously hadn't known she'd returned.

She sat on the bottom step of the stairs and looked up through half closed eyes, 'Shall I get my papers?' she asked sleepily.

'Er, no, that won't be necessary. Did any of you hear the van which was reported as having stopped down the road?'

Dr Gaston and Genevieve both pretended to think carefully and then shook their heads.

'Well, if you hear anything that would be useful to our enquiries, let us know.'

'Of course,' Dr Gaston said, closing the door.

'You must be careful, Angelique. If someone was watching and reported the van, we may be under suspicion, despite the officer seeming to have believed us.'

She nodded. 'Yes, I'll be careful.'

'Goodnight, then,' he said, going towards his bedroom. 'And well done!'

* * *

Genevieve heard nothing from Marcel, Henri or Yves for two days.

She wandered past the Café Fleur de Lys in the square and stopped outside, pretending to rummage in her handbag for something but really glancing

185

sideways to see if anyone she knew was inside. The café owner, seeing her outside, grabbed a tray and cloth and hurried to the table closest to the window where she was standing. He placed the empty cups on the tray and, with his back to his customers, made eye contact with her. Frowning, he imperceptibly shook his head.

She gave a tiny nod to show she'd understood his warning not to enter and as he vigorously cleaned the table with his cloth, she walked on. Obviously, the café was being watched.

Patients waiting to see Dr Gaston often gossiped about what was happening in their community and Genevieve hung on to the hope that since no one had said anyone had been arrested for the explosion, then Marcel, Henri and Yves were safe. She'd even mentioned to one of Dr Gaston's regular visitors, Madame Lavaud that she could still detect the smell of burnt wood in the air and hoped it would prompt some comments from the woman.

It did. Madame Lavaud's cousin had worked at the factory and she expressed relief that he'd escaped with his life and then talked at length about how shocked he and his wife had been.

'I thought the explosion took place at night,' Genevieve said, not wanting to hear about the cousin or his wife and her nervous disposition.

'Well, yes, I believe it did. But nevertheless — '

'D'you think they've caught anyone?'

'I don't believe so. I've got another cousin who works in the office at the police station. If they'd arrested anyone, she'd have told me, I'm sure . . . d'you think Dr Gaston will be much longer?'

That seemed to be as much as Madame Lavaud could tell her but at least it gave Genevieve hope.

Shortly after she'd gone in to see Dr Gaston, a man entered. It was Marcel!

'Good morning, Monsieur, how may I help?'

'Good morning, Mademoiselle, I wonder if it would be possible to make an appointment to see Dr Gaston today?'

'Hmm,' she said, running her finger down the appointment slots in the book, 'I can fit you in.'

As soon as Madame Lavaud came out of Dr Gaston's surgery, Genevieve rushed in before the next patient and explained that Marcel would be coming to see him.

'It must be a message for you, Angelique,' Dr Gaston said. 'Make sure to bring him in here and then stay.'

Genevieve followed Marcel into the doctor's room, as instructed.

'Yves wants you to be ready to leave at first light tomorrow morning, Angelique,' Marcel said once he'd shaken hands with Dr Gaston, 'He doesn't know how long we'll be away.'

'Where are we going?' she asked.

'Somewhere south of Paris. You'll be travelling with my uncle in his truck. He's going to take vegetables to market in Paris and he'll drop you off on the way.'

Genevieve waited in the shadow of the tree in the front garden the following morning and as soon as the truck pulled up, she climbed in. She felt a rush of pleasure at seeing Yves again and he seemed unusually pleased to see her.

'Where's Henri?' she asked.

'He's staying here. Marcel is planning a raid on an ammo dump further south and needs supplies from London. Henri's coordinating everything. This job won't need more than two people.'

'So, what is it?'

'A rescue attempt.'

'Who are we going to rescue?'

'With any luck, your brother.'

It was several moments before Genevieve could speak. 'How . . . ?' she finally managed.

'Marcel made enquiries. We've located your brother. He was captured and taken to Fresnes Prison, but for some reason he's been taken to a smaller prison. One of the guards is a sympathiser and said he'll help us get Jean-Paul out.'

'Why would he do that?'

'He wants payment and safe passage out of the country. That's his price. So, we'll pass him on to another group along with your brother and get them both over the demarcation line into the Free Zone. Another group will get them across the Pyrenees. It'll take a while and it'll be risky but it may be your brother's only chance . . . ' Yves paused and placed his hand over Genevieve's, 'We don't think he's in a good way. They were all badly treated in Fresnes . . . '

Genevieve swallowed her tears, not wanting to think about her brother in pain.

Marcel's uncle dropped them off close to the prison and arranged to meet them at the same place at six o'clock that evening.

'I won't be able to wait if you're not here,' he said, 'but I'll be back on Wednesday.'

In the prison, Yves asked for Sergeant Dufour and a small, nervous-looking man led them into an office. With his darting, suspicious eyes, he reminded Genevieve of a rat.

'Do you have the money?' he asked.

'We want to see the prisoner first,' Yves said.

Taking a bunch of keys from his desk, he led them from his office down some stone steps to the cells in the basement.

'I'm sorry you have to see this, Angelique,' Yves said, putting his arm around her shoulders, 'but we need to know if this man really is your brother.' He bent closer to Genevieve and whispered, 'I don't trust him at all.'

Genevieve shook her head. 'Me neither.'

Ahead of them the sergeant opened the door and beckoned them forward. Genevieve took a deep breath. Part of her hoped it was JP, while the other part dreaded seeing him injured or hurt.

191

She peered into the gloomy cell and gasped. The pain of seeing her emaciated, bruised brother shackled to the wall was agony! She tried to rush to him, but the sergeant put his arm out and stopped her. He was surprisingly strong for such a small, wiry man.

'I want the money first.'

Genevieve pushed past the restraining arm and knelt by JP, speaking to him softly. He looked up but didn't seem to recognise her and his head flopped to one side as if it was too much effort to hold it up. Genevieve looked up at Yves, silently imploring him to do something.

'Can you get him out of this cell now?' Yves asked. 'I have all the money you asked for,' he added quickly.

'No, there are too many people on duty now. Come back at four. I brought some bottles of wine for the guards and I'll make sure they have a long lunch. There's a door at the back of the prison. I'll bring him out through that.'

Yves nodded. 'Agreed.'

'Money,' the sergeant said, greedily holding out his hand.

'Not until he's out,' Yves said.

'How do I know I can trust you?'

'You don't, but I'm a man of my word. I will pay you and I will get you out of France. But I need to know this man is safe first.'

The sergeant thought for a moment and then quickly nodded his head. 'Go to the back of the prison. I'll meet you there with the prisoner. As soon as we're outside, I want my money.'

Genevieve gently kissed JP's forehead and stood up. 'Give him something to eat,' she said to the sergeant.

* * *

Once they left the prison, they bought food for the journey and a suit for JP. Genevieve alternated between elation at the thought that her brother would soon be free, and fear that the sergeant would double-cross them. The sight of JP so weak and thin, with hollow

193

unseeing eyes, haunted her. The minutes until they would meet him dragged and she repeatedly checked her watch but time seemed to have almost stopped.

Yves and Genevieve arrived slightly early, not wanting to be seen loitering for too long, but the door remained locked.

'D'you think he came out before we got here?' Genevieve asked, her voice breaking as she fought back her tears.

'No, he wants the money and he needs us if he's to stand a chance of escaping. He'd have waited until we came.'

Genevieve checked her watch again and noticing the silver heart hanging from the bracelet, she held it between her finger and thumb, silently invoking the good luck which Sonny had believed the charm would bring.

The scraping of the bolt against the lock made her jump. Immediately, she and Yves were alert and ready to react to whoever opened the door.

It was the sergeant, dressed in worker's clothes with a cloth cap and a bag over his shoulder. He guided JP out of the gate and Yves supported his weight as they made their escape.

They hid in a derelict house where they dressed JP in the new suit and fed him. He was ravenous but Genevieve gave him small amounts to allow his stomach to get used to eating again after the meagre rations he'd obviously been given.

At six o'clock, they were waiting for Marcel's uncle at the agreed rendez-vous but there was no sign of him. Had he got there early and not waited? Genevieve could feel waves of panic rise through her. Surely, they hadn't got this far only to be picked up for loitering?

'That's him!' Yves said, hailing the lorry to make sure he stopped.

'Sorry I'm late. I've been searched at every roadblock this side of Paris!' Marcel's uncle grumbled. 'Best get in the back and hide behind all the crates. If the next lot of soldiers are as thorough, we're going to be in trouble.'

At the next checkpoint, the solder glanced in the rear at the empty vegetable boxes and remarked that it must have been a profitable day for Marcel's uncle, who agreed that it had.

'So . . . ' the soldier said, expectantly, keeping hold of the identity papers.

Marcel's uncle sighed, reached into his pocket for some Francs which he passed to the soldier who pretended to consider if there was enough for him to hand the documents back. When a few more notes were added, he passed the identity papers back and waved the lorry through. After that, luck was with them and after a quick glance in the back, guards allowed the lorry though.

* * *

'The bruising and cuts will heal and there's no lasting damage to his body but obviously, he needs plenty of food and rest before he's strong enough to venture out,' Dr Gaston said to Genevieve after examining JP.

Yves had helped carry JP into the doctor's house and upstairs. Then he'd taken the prison sergeant to the Escoffier's house where later, Marcel had arrived in his van. They escorted the runaway sergeant to Blois and handed him over to their contact in the Sapphire Circuit. The following day, he would be moved towards the demarcation line and passed on to another circuit until eventually, he would be led across the Pyrenees to Spain.

'I'd like to have wrung his neck!' Marcel said once they'd transferred the sergeant to their contact in Sapphire. 'My uncle told me what sort of state Angelique's brother was in. That sergeant doesn't deserve anyone to put their life in danger for him.'

'At least we saved one man,' Yves said, 'And someone very special to Angelique.'

★　★　★

Blanche took over from Genevieve when she fell into an exhausted sleep after having watched over her brother for several days. His bruises were fading and the colour had returned to his cheeks, although they were still hollow and his bones clearly defined.

The rations for three people in the house had to be shared between four — one of whom needed more than an average adult meal — and Genevieve often went without food so her brother could eat well. She knew both Dr Gaston and his wife did the same, stretching their food allowance to the limit.

Marcel brought vegetables which his uncle provided for them and Yves arrived one day with cream and cheese from the Escoffiers.

Genevieve was so relieved to see the withdrawn skeleton they'd first brought home fill out and return to the brother she recognised, although she knew that as long as he remained in the Gaston house, her hosts were in danger. If the house was searched by the authorities, it wouldn't be possible to hide JP in time and they'd all be seized and charged with harbouring a fugitive. As soon as he was able to walk, he'd need to be sent home. But how long would it be before he'd be able to make the exhausting journey on foot over the Pyrenees?

She told Yves how worried she was that it might take months for him to regain the strength needed to cross the mountains and, in the meantime, her friends were in danger while he was in their house.

'I've been thinking about that and I've decided we're not going send him across the Pyrenees,' Yves said.

'He can't stay here!' Genevieve was aghast.

Had they got him out of prison, fed him up until he was well, only to keep him here a virtual prisoner? Or worse, until he was captured again?

'Of course not. As soon as he's well, Henri will request London sends a plane to come and take him home.'

'Will the SOE do that?'

'Yes. He's one of theirs and now he's in trouble, I believe they'll do all they can to get him home. Trust me. Henri's already informed London he's here and as soon as you think he's strong enough to make the journey, we'll organise it.'

Genevieve threw her arms about Yves' neck and hugged him tightly. For a second, he held her too — and then gently disengaged himself.

'Just let me know when you think he'll be able to travel,' he said.

★ ★ ★

'When you get back — '

'Yes, I know, Pipsqueak, I'll ask if the BBC will broadcast my message to let you know I've arrived safely,' JP said to Genevieve, hugging her tightly. 'And thank you . . .'

Above them, the Lysander aircraft, small and black, glided overhead. With his torch, Yves flashed the agreed code into the night sky and the pilot replied to signal he would land on the improvised airstrip indicated by strategically placed torches. The plane came in for a bumpy landing on the field and eventually halted yards from the waiting group.

A man emerged from the rear cockpit, climbed down the ladder and ran towards them while JP hurried to take his place. Once inside, the pilot waved and turned round, ready to taxi across the grass and rise up into the darkness heading towards England.

The man who'd arrived was immediately taken by members of the Monarch Circuit — he was the replacement for their wireless operator who'd been arrested.

'Is Estelle still with you?' Genevieve asked, hoping desperately that her friend Nathalie, alias Estelle, was safe. The men said she was and Genevieve asked if they'd let her know Angelique had asked after her. It was the first contact she'd had with the girl she'd trained with since she'd been in France and with the knowledge that her brother had just flown to safety, Genevieve felt a great weight lift from her. She was so wrapped up in her thoughts, it took a second to realise bullets were whistling past her!

Yves grabbed her arm and both bent double as they ran to the hedge and slipped through, rushing for the van that was waiting for them.

'Go! Go! Go!' Yves yelled and Marcel slammed his foot on the accelerator, flinging them all forward. Ahead of them, the men from Monarch Circuit had heard the gunfire and were speeding away. At the crossroads, the Monarch people swung to the left while Marcel turned right, making for the Escoffier farm.

When they reached the barn, Yves and Genevieve leaped out and opened the door beckoning Marcel forward until the van was inside, then Henri joined them in closing the door.

'There must've been a leak,' Marcel

said, his hand was shaking as he lit a Gauloises and took a long drag.

'Surely not,' said Henri. 'The soldiers might have been on patrol and seen the aircraft. It could just be a coincidence.'

'I don't believe in coincidences,' said Marcel, 'I'll see if anyone knows what's going on.'

'Is there anything we can do?' Henri asked.

Yves thought for a moment and sadly shook his head, 'All we can do is try to signal to the others if something's wrong. For now, keep something large, like a vase or desk lamp, in the window of your bedroom as a sign all's well and if . . . if things go wrong and you get the chance, remove it. Other than that,' Yves said, 'we all have to be extra vigilant and take care.'

Genevieve thought that, if someone had betrayed the members of the circuit, then they wouldn't know who was watching them nor when they would strike. The thought that someone she knew had informed the Germans about the Tulip Circuit wiped out her earlier optimism, leaving her with a terrible feeling of foreboding.

* * *

The following evening, Henri, Marcel, Genevieve and Yves gathered around the wireless set in Madame Escoffier's kitchen listening for the BBC Personal Messages after the news.

'Before we begin, please listen to some personal messages . . . ' the BBC presenter said, 'I found a diamond ring in a cake . . . A blackbird is nesting in the tree outside the window . . . Please take care, it's very muddy . . . Theseus tells Pipsqueak he's escaped from the labyrinth . . . '

'Yes!' said Genevieve, so excited she stood up, tipping her chair over backwards, 'That's the code! My brother's home safely!'

The men turned away and pretended not to notice when tears trickled down her cheeks.

The following day, Genevieve cycled to the crossroads where she waited for Marcel to arrive in his van. Beneath the bottles of pills and medicines in the bicycle basket, she'd packed a few clothes and her toiletries in a bag in case she needed to stay away for several nights.

When the van stopped, Yves got out and helped her hide her bicycle with his, beneath the firewood in the back.

They'd had word from the Crescent Circuit that an airman who'd been shot down near Le Mans needed to be flown back to England. If he'd been well, he'd have made the arduous journey across the Pyrenees to Spain, but this man had been badly wounded in the crash and had required more medical care than the Crescent Circuit could provide. They'd contacted London who'd agreed to send a plane, as they'd done for JP, but the anti-aircraft fire near the circuit's makeshift runway had proved too much for the tiny Lysander aircraft and it had been unable to land.

To make matters worse, Crescent's wireless operator had been picked up by one of the German Radio Direction Finder vans which had been sweeping Le Mans. They were neither able to contact London to request a new operator and wireless set, nor to arrange transportation for their wounded pilot.

Yves had agreed that he and Genevieve would leave Marcel outside the village. They would then cycle to the address they'd been given and see if the pilot was well enough to travel with them in the van or if they should delay a few days for him to gather his strength. Marcel would wait for them until six o'clock, then leave if they weren't there.

Genevieve and Yves arrived at the address and gave the password to the anxious woman who peered out through a crack in the door. She quickly ushered them inside, glancing nervously up the road. 'I'm afraid you've had a wasted journey,' she said. 'The pilot died half an hour ago. But please let London know we're without a wireless operator.'

Yves promised to pass the message on to Henri for him to include in his sched that evening and they left soon after, hurrying back to Marcel.

They were all silent on the way home.

Yet another young man dead because of this cruel, senseless war, Genevieve thought, thanking God once again that JP had made it home.

As they pulled into the street where Henri rented a room, Genevieve looked up at his window.

'Yves!' she said, 'Look!'

Yves looked up at the bare window. When he'd passed the day before, there'd been a desk lamp visible, but now it had gone.

'Keep driving, Marcel!' Yves said.

'My friend's mother lives almost opposite, I'll park the van round the corner and see if she knows anything,' said Marcel. He returned ten minutes later, his head down, hurrying.

'Soldiers raided his building this morning,' he said, quickly putting the van in gear and accelerating down the road.

'Did they get Henri?' Yves asked.

'She didn't know. Several men were taken away but she couldn't see who they were.'

At the crossroads, Yves and Genevieve unloaded their bicycles and Marcel drove off to see what he could find out about the raid on Henri's apartment building.

They wheeled their bicycles along the road to Dr Gaston's house. Other than Madame Lavaud who was coming towards them, no one was lurking.

'Oh, Mademoiselle!' Madame Lavaud said, raising her hands in a gesture of helplessness, 'Whatever next!'

'What's the matter?' Genevieve asked.

'It's just too much! Taking away our doctor like that — and his wife as well!'

208

'Dr Gaston's been taken away?' Genevieve asked, incredulously.

'It was most unpleasant! The . . . ' she lowered her voice and whispered, 'The Gestapo, arrived and searched the house, then took poor Dr Gaston and his wife away! It was terrifying! I've been at my sister's ever since. I was frightened to go home. But my husband will be back soon and I need to prepare supper.'

'Thank you for telling me, Madame,' Genevieve said as the woman walked away, shaking her head as if she couldn't believe it.

'You can't go home,' said Yves. 'They'll be watching Henri's room and Dr Gaston's house. You'd better come to the Escoffier's with me.'

They cycled towards the farm but dismounted and after leaving their bicycles hidden in a ditch, they continued on foot across the fields. In the farmyard, a military vehicle was parked and the sound of smashing furniture and crashing crockery carried across the field. If they'd needed any more warning, the large vase Yves had placed on the table in front of his window was gone.

Yves caught Genevieve's hand and pulled her away, back to the bicycles.

'Where can we go?' she asked, gasping to catch her breath as they ran.

'I don't know. It looks like someone's betrayed Tulip Circuit. And if they've got information about us, they'll probably know all our safe houses and be watching them.'

They mounted their bicycles and rode as fast as they could away from the farm. Skirting the town, Yves finally stopped in a wood to rest.

'We could go back to my grandfather's cave,' Genevieve suggested. 'It's not comfortable but no one would think to look for us there.'

Yves chewed his bottom lip, considering her suggestion. He was about to agree, when she said, 'No! I know where we can go! My uncle lives on a farm in Normandy. He'll take us in.'

4

That evening Yves and Genevieve arrived in a tiny village in the middle of the Norman countryside, half way between Bayeux and the coast. They'd found a lorry driver who'd taken them as far as Alençon, then another who dropped them on the outskirts of Bayeux. From there, they'd cycled ten miles to the Vannier's farm.

Uncle Alexandre was closing the large wooden gates into the farmyard for the evening when the two weary cyclists arrived and it had taken him several moments to recognise his niece.

'Genevieve? Chérie! What are you doing here? Come in! Come in!' He glanced warily up and down the road and then quickly closed the gates and led them to the large, stone farmhouse. 'Denise! Gabrielle! Come and see who's here!'

Aunt Denise, small, round and with brown curls framing her smiling face appeared in the hall, her hands covered in flour. 'Mon Dieu! Genevieve! What are you doing here? I thought you were safe in England.' She kissed her niece on both cheeks, then holding her at arms' length, she looked at her with delight and fear in her eyes.

A younger, slimmer version of Denise appeared at the top of the stairs, rushing down the steps and kissed her cousin.

'And who's your young man?' Denise asked, leading them into the large farm kitchen.

While they had coffee, Genevieve told them about being placed in France by the SOE and working in the Tulip Circuit with local French Resistance workers. Genevieve could tell from Yves' expression he wasn't happy about her revealing details to her family, but if they were going to throw themselves on the Vanniers' mercy and ask for a place to stay until they could contact other

212

resisters in Normandy, they needed to understand the risks.

'It may be that I can help you,' Alexandre said, pouring each person a glass of homemade Calvados, the fiery apple brandy they made on the farm. 'I have contacts in the local Resistance. In fact, from time to time, we've had SOE agents and RAF airmen staying here on their way to safety.'

'There's obviously something in the Vannier family blood to fight for freedom,' Denise said, 'Your parents are helping the Free French in London, and I suspected Jean-Paul was in France but I had no idea you were here too!'

Genevieve could see Yves begin to relax as he learned of her family's involvement with the fight against the Nazis.

'If only Grand-père were free,' Genevieve said sadly, explaining how she and Yves had seen Château Saint Pierre overrun with Germans. 'He didn't look well and — oh, Oncle

213

Alexandre, if you'd seen him! He was limping, and so thin. The officer threatened to shoot the dogs.'

Alexandre gripped the edge of the table until his knuckles turned white. Remembering her uncle had once argued intensely with her grandfather, Genevieve wondered if she'd made a mistake in mentioning him, that memories of his father had angered him. But Alexandre had never been vindictive and the dispute now took second place to the thought that his father was being abused at the hands of their oppressors. This dreadful war was a time for families to come together, not to remember petty grievances from the past.

Gabrielle set the table for dinner. Denise removed the apple tart from the oven and checked the stew for seasoning, while Alexandre questioned the two guests about his father.

In the farmyard, the dogs began howling and Alexandre ran to the window. 'Someone's opening the gates!

Quick, take them upstairs! You know what to do!'

Denise seized the two plates and cutlery she'd set for her guests and pushed them back into the cupboard, making it look like there were only three people ready to dine while Alexandre went out into the farmyard to quieten the dogs.

None of their neighbours would come this late and Alexandre's suspicions it might be someone official proved to be correct. Out in the farmyard, he saw a truck, a German officer inside. When he saw Alexandre, he climbed out of the vehicle and with an imperious wave of his hand, indicated the driver should advance into the farmyard.

'Wait for me here,' he said. 'I am Hauptmann Werner Reinhold. I have been informed you have two strangers in your house.'

Alexandre shook his head slowly. 'No, just my wife, my daughter and me.'

'Really . . . ?' Hauptmann Reinhold

tapped his leather boot with his swagger stick. 'How strange, because someone reported seeing two cyclists stop at your gate and then enter.'

'Oh yes . . . ' Alexandre checked his watch. 'About an hour ago. They were lost, so I offered to draw them a map and explain the route. You know how easy it is to get lost with all these narrow lanes. They left, cycling towards the coast.'

'I see . . . Nevertheless, I will have to follow up the report. My informant did not mention anything about them leaving. So, I'm sure you won't mind if my men and I search your house . . . '

'That's not convenient, I'm afraid. My wife's about to serve dinner . . . '

'Excellent. Tell her to set another place for me while my men search the house.'

★   ★   ★

'My compliments, Madame,' Hauptmann Reinhard said to Denise as he placed his knife and fork on the plate. 'How lucky I arrived just in time for freshly baked apple tart. I have to say that despite the rations, you managed to produce a delicious meal . . . unless you have dealings with the black market . . . I hope that is not the case.'

'Certainly not!' she said rising and clearing the plates quickly, in the hope the captain would go.

'Coffee would be lovely,' the captain said.

Denise nodded at Gabrielle to make him coffee.

'It's rather weak for my taste,' he said when he sipped the drink she placed in front of him.

'Coffee is on ration,' Denise snapped. 'That's the best we can do.' She knew Gabrielle had deliberately added more water and silently congratulated her daughter.

When he'd finished the coffee, the Vannier family sat silently, waiting for their unwelcome visitor to go. Finally, he rose, clicked his heels and raised his arm in a Nazi salute. He walked to the door, then turned to the family. 'I shall leave a man here tonight . . . just as a precaution, you understand. Those strangers may get lost again and return for directions. I would be very interested to talk to them. I shall return tomorrow.'

A soldier came into the kitchen and sat at the table while Denise cleared the plates. Alexandre placed a glass and bottle of Calvados on the table in front of the soldier. Denise shot her husband a furious look and then softened when she realised he was hoping the soldier would drink too much. It was easy to do, as the apple brandy was very potent. While her husband poured a large glassful and explained to the soldier how it was made, she hid bread, cheese, ham and a bottle of cider in her sewing basket which she planned to take upstairs for Genevieve and Yves.

'What is that, Madame?' the soldier asked pointing at the sewing basket.

'This?' she asked innocently, 'Just my

sewing. I always tidy up before bedtime.'

Hiding her anger with a smile, she placed the basket on the shelf, as if she really had been clearing away. Now she wouldn't be able to take them anything to eat. If she attempted to take the basket upstairs, she risked the soldier insisting on looking inside.

Genevieve and Yves were hiding in a small bedroom concealed behind Gabrielle's room. A false wall had been built with a door concealed in one of the panels. In front of that, a chest of drawers stood. It was in this hidden room that the SOE agents and RAF men had been kept for a night or two before being passed on. Someone must be suspicious about their clandestine work to have reported two cyclists, Denise thought with a shiver of fear that someone — possibly one of their neighbours — had been so malicious.

She waited outside the hidden room, listening for the sound of her husband's footsteps on the stone stairs. While he remained downstairs, she knew the soldier was there too and with Gabrielle's help, she gently lifted the chest of drawers and moved it so she could open the door a fraction to whisper that the officer had gone but he'd left a man downstairs. Then just as quietly, they moved the chest of drawers back in position.

*   *   *

Other than two skylights in the roof, there were no windows in the secret room. It was sparsely furnished with one double bed and a small table on which was a bottle of Calvados — opened, possibly by the last occupant. Next to the table, was an upright, wooden chair. There was little space for anything else. The room had obviously been designed for secrecy, not comfort.

Denise's news that the officer had left a guard downstairs was not welcome. She'd also explained that as a result, she'd be unable to bring food for them but, if at all possible, she'd smuggle something up later. It had been hours since they'd had breakfast and now Genevieve's stomach growled hungrily. They both sat silent, straining to hear anything which might indicate another search was being carried out.

Genevieve was worried about her family. She'd unwittingly brought danger to their house. While considering Yves' comfort she'd suggested coming to Normandy as an alternative to hiding in a cave but now, they were both hungry and confined to a tiny room which was lit only by the moon. It seemed her plan, well meant as it had been, had benefited no one.

'We might as well try and get some sleep,' Yves said, 'You take the bed.'

'You can't spend the night sitting in that chair. You won't sleep a wink and we need to be fresh for tomorrow. We're both adults, we should be able to sleep in the same bed.'

He smiled. 'It's because we're adults

that we shouldn't sleep in the same bed.'

'How about I sleep under the bedclothes and you stay on top?'

'That might work,' he said. 'I'm sure the blanket will ensure I keep my hands off you . . . '

'Oh, stop teasing,' she said. 'It's not like we haven't spent the night together before.'

'That's true. We spent two nights under a parachute, as I recall. It was itchy and cold in that hay loft. And a night in a cave. That was also very uncomfortable. I seem to remember I was savaged by a lizard. I have to say, sleeping with you is always memorable.'

'Oh, very amusing! I'm glad you can see the funny side of things,' she said. 'I was feeling guilty about having brought you here.'

'Why? It looks like it's going to be a comfortable night, even if I have to share the bed with you!'

Despite his joking, Genevieve could see he was ill-at-ease.

'How about a nightcap?' she suggested. 'At least it'll make our stomachs think we haven't forgotten them.' She took the bottle of Calvados and pulled out the cork, then swallowing a mouthful, she nearly choked, 'That's strong stuff!' she gasped, 'Now I know why my parents never let me have any when I was young. It seems to be going straight to my head.' She handed him the bottle.

'It's definitely got a kick,' Yves said, after taking a mouthful and giving it back to her.

For someone with such self-confidence and nerve, he seemed remarkably embarrassed, Genevieve thought.

They passed the bottle back and forth, taking sips of the strong liquid.

Yves turned his back while she undressed, folded her clothes and got into bed. She didn't know when she'd get clean clothes again and when they eventually were able to leave the Vanniers' farm, she didn't want to arouse suspicion by looking as if she'd been sleeping rough.

She remembered her SOE training and the alcohol she'd drunk then with the blessing of the trainers who'd watched to ensure it didn't make their students too talkative. It hadn't affected her as much as many of the others, but now the Calvados was making the ceiling spin. The fiery spirit glowed inside her, taking away the gnawing hunger. Thankfully, it was also blunting her embarrassment at the being so close to Yves.

As he'd pointed out, they'd both spent several nights together but somehow, faced with the prospect of sharing a bed, she was nervous. Not because she thought he'd do anything she didn't want — she trusted him implicitly — but because the bed represented a degree of intimacy which she'd never before shared with Yves.

The first few nights after she'd landed in France, when they'd slept in the hay loft, she hadn't known him at all but she'd been aware of his hostility.

Later, in the cave, she knew he'd accepted her as a fellow operative and she'd realised how much she enjoyed his company. But now, the more time she spent with him alone, the more she was drawn to him. She trusted him, relied on him, and despite her best efforts, she suspected she was falling in love with him.

This evening before the German officer and his men had arrived, she'd watched Yves talking to her uncle over coffee. The two men seemed to have taken an instant liking to each other and Genevieve allowed herself the brief fantasy of normality — letting herself dream the world was at peace and that she and Yves were visiting her family, just like any other girl might take her sweetheart to meet her relatives.

The two men had discussed farming and apple crops and Yves told her uncle about his father's land and the problems he'd encountered. She'd watched Yves' animation and the way he ran his hands through his blonde fringe, brushing it back like he did when he was engrossed. She loved his grey eyes crinkling at the corners when he smiled. And that smile which made her knees weak . . .

The reverie had ended abruptly when the dogs started barking at the arrival of the Germans.

She realised she'd allowed herself to slip into an unreal world where it was possible that she and Yves might be together. She'd let herself imagine being with him, holding him and lying next to him in bed — without a blanket between them. She needed to rein in her imagination and banish all thoughts of closeness with Yves. He'd made it clear she was a comrade-in-arms, a trusted aide but nothing more and when he'd held her tightly or inter-twined his fingers with hers, it was only to throw the Germans off their scent.

She welcomed the warm glow the Calvados induced. It blurred the lines of reality and with any luck, it would numb them both enough to be able to sleep in the same bed.

But obviously not yet.

Yves sat on the bed, leaning against the headboard, his body rigid with tension. To try to relax him, she asked about his life in England before the war had broken out. Gradually, as the moon moved across one of the skylights, disappeared and then became visible in the other, he began to unwind as they talked.

The bottle now stood empty on the table.

'You know,' he said, loosening the collar of his shirt and sliding down the bed. 'When I realised London had sent me a girl, I was really upset, but I have to admit, you have your good points. Of course, you have bad points too.'

'Really?' she said with mock affront, 'And what are they?'

'That you're devilishly attractive and all my men find you too distracting for words.'

She giggled. 'I see. And my good points?'

'That you're devilishly attractive and German soldiers find you too distracting for words.'

Neither of them was too drunk to be unaware of the soldier downstairs, nor of the danger they were in, but under the influence of the apple brandy it was easy to pretend they were old friends teasing each other because the alternative was the embarrassing awkwardness they'd experienced earlier.

'Do my good points outweigh my bad points?'

'It's hard to say.'

'Why's that?'

'Because you're devilishly attractive and I find you too distracting to make up my mind!'

Genevieve giggled and Yves suppressed his laughter. He reached out and placed a finger on her lips to signal they must remain quiet.

In an instant, the atmosphere changed from one of tipsy camaraderie to something electrifying. Their eyes locked and, keeping his finger on her lips, Yves began to trace the outline of her mouth, sending shockwaves of pleasure radiating through her body. He let his finger gently follow the contours of her chin, down to the hollow at the base of her neck. Leaning towards her, he brushed her lips with his. She gasped and placed her hands behind his head, pulling him towards her, eager to press her lips to his.

Both Eric and Sonny had kissed her but she had never experienced anything like Yves' Calvados-sweet kisses. Neither had anything prepared her for the feelings diffusing throughout her body, making her feel as if she were floating on air.

She pulled him closer. He slid down the bed, lying alongside her and she wriggled free of the blanket, wanting to feel the warmth of his body.

'Angelique,' he whispered in her ear.

His breath felt delicious against her neck as his lips glided across her skin, down her neck, leaving butterfly kisses. She gasped with pleasure.

Undoing the buttons of his shirt, she breathed in the faintest scent of sandalwood, then slipped her hands inside, smoothing her fingers over the contours of his muscles. She'd never seen him without a shirt but now, although the moonlight was bright enough to make him out, she didn't need to see him as her hands explored and she committed it all to memory.

The tap at the door was gentle but loud enough to stop them.

They froze, listening.

Yves leaped off the bed just as Denise opened the door slightly and passed in a bundle.

'Some food,' she whispered 'The guard is drunk downstairs. I'll let you know when it's safe to come out.'

The door closed quietly and Genevieve heard her aunt and cousin whispering as they replaced the chest of drawers over the door.

Yves opened the cloth to find cheese, ham, bread and a bottle of cider which he shared with Genevieve.

'I'm so sorry, Angelique,' he said, sitting on the bed with his back to her, 'I've behaved unacceptably.'

Genevieve said nothing. Unacceptably? He thought he'd behaved unacceptably! How could he describe what they'd just experienced as unacceptable?

They ate in silence. The food was welcome but tasted of nothing. Later when they lay down — she under the blanket and he on top with his back to her — her stomach churned with nausea.

★ ★ ★

The guard snored, arms cushioning his head on the table when Denise went down to the kitchen in the morning. She made as much noise as she could, rattling plates and cutlery and slamming the kettle down on the hob with a crash. Even so, it took a few minutes for the guard to wake. He groaned as he sat up and rubbed his neck, moving his

231

head from side to side trying to ease the ache. 'Bonjour, Madame,' he said politely and then added in French, 'I wonder if I could trouble you for a glass of water?'

'Your French is very good,' she said.

He blushed, 'My maternal grandmother is French. I spent many summers in Paris with her.'

How ironic that this boy — for Denise conceded, he was still only a boy — was part of the army now occupying his own grandmother's country. The previous evening when he'd questioned what she was doing with her sewing basket, he'd spoken imperiously, with authority conferred by his officer's dogged determination to serve the Reich. Now, hungover and sitting in a French kitchen possibly similar to his grandmother's the self-importance and brashness had gone.

Nevertheless, he's still a danger to us Denise reminded herself. She made him a large cup of strong coffee and cut a small slice off the loaf of bread, putting it in front of him with some of the creamy butter she made on the farm.

Her act of generosity made him hang his head as he mumbled his thanks.

When Gabrielle appeared, Denise looked at her daughter, silently imploring her not to comment on the fact their precious rations were once again being wasted on a member of the Boche.

'Shall I milk the cows for you today, Maman?' she asked, making it obvious from her curled lip she didn't want to be anywhere near the soldier for a moment longer than necessary.

'Papa has gone to do it, thank you chérie, but if you could feed the chickens and fetch the eggs, I would be very grateful, thank you.' She turned back to the soldier. 'What I don't understand is why your captain thought there was anyone here other than my husband, daughter and myself.' She shook her head in pained disbelief.

While she didn't hold out much hope he knew anything and much less he'd tell her, it was worth a try.

'Madame, I believe one of your neighbours reported seeing two people come into the farm.'

'Now why would anyone do that?' she said, as if musing to herself. 'We get on so well with our neighbours. I simply cannot understand why someone would try to stir up trouble so wilfully.'

'I believe the man does not live in the village.'

'Then who could it be?'

'I don't know his name.'

'Oh,' she said, as if close to tears.

'But you may recognise him,' the soldier said. 'He is a small man. Smaller than me and he has a black moustache, a bit like our Führer, except bigger and bushy, and he keeps scratching it.'

'Has he got a gold tooth?'

'Yes! Do you know him?' the soldier asked.

'I most certainly do! It sounds like Monsieur Albin!' Denise said, outraged.

'That explains it.'

'What does it explain, Madame?'

'Monsieur Albin came several hours before you and your captain trying to sell us his black-market goods and I turned him away. He was very angry and Monsieur Albin is a man to bear a grudge.'

This was in fact true. Denise had turned him away and his last words had been that she would regret treating him without respect. Now she knew who'd reported them, how to ensure the captain didn't leave another guard with them?

'More coffee, young man?' she asked.

'No, thank you. You have been very kind, Madame, and I'm sorry you've been inconvenienced because of that man's vindictiveness.' The soldier pressed his lips together and looked at her fearfully. 'I . . . I wonder if I could ask a . . . a favour of you?'

'Well, you can ask, I suppose.'

'When Hauptmann Reinhold returns today, I wonder if you could . . . ' He glanced at the empty Calvados bottle. ' . . . That is, I wonder if you . . . '

The sound of the dogs barking prevented him finishing his sentence and he gulped down the last of his coffee.

'Wait!' Denise said. 'Your top button is undone. Straighten your uniform or you'll get into trouble!' She pointed at the mirror hanging on the wall and he quickly smartened himself up, then putting on his cap and slinging his rifle over his shoulder, he marched outside.

Hauptmann Reinhold remained in the truck while the two farm dogs ran back and forth barking madly. Denise called them to heel and, with tongues hanging out, they ran to her side, waiting for the word to rush at the intruders. The officer got out of his car, glowering at the dogs.

Taking the initiative, Denise said, 'I wish to complain in the strongest possible terms, Herr Hauptmann.'

'And why is that, Madame?'

'That soldier,' she said pointing at the

boy who'd been in her house all night. He blanched and began to stutter something but Denise held up her hand and continued, 'I've hardly had a moment's sleep with him walking up and down stairs and patrolling all over the house. I've already told you you're wasting your time here. But no! He's been poking his nose into everything.'

'Really?' Hauptmann Reinhold tapped his boot with his swagger stick and contemplated the red-cheeked boy.

'And did you find anything, Horst?'

'Nein, Herr Hauptmann, nothing at all.' Private Horst had obviously caught on that the more Denise complained about him and claimed he'd been diligent during the night, the more impressed Hauptmann Reinhold would be.

'I see . . . in that case, Madame, may I offer you my apologies for any inconvenience.' The officer clicked his fingers to indicate Horst should get into the back of the truck.

'By the way, Herr Hauptmann,'

Denise said, 'you expressed a dislike of the black market when you were here yesterday.'

'Yes. That is true.'

'Well, several hours before you arrived I was threatened by a black marketeer because I would not buy his goods. I thought you should be aware.'

'Do you have any names?'

'Yesterday a man called Albin — '

'Does this man have a rather absurd bushy moustache and a gold tooth at the front?'

'Why yes — do you know him? He came here yesterday and when I wouldn't buy from him he said I'd regret it.'

The officer's eyes narrowed and his swagger stick twitched irritably.

'Leave it with me, Madame. Please be assured this man will not trouble you again.'

Denise placed a hand on each of the dogs' heads and watched as the truck pulled out of the yard. Her morning's work on the farm hadn't yet begun yet already she'd got rid of the Germans and that nasty man, Albin. Lies. All lies.

Well, all except Monsieur Albin having tried to sell them black market goods — and now she'd betrayed him to the Germans. At least, Hauptmann Reinhold would believe they were innocent and had been victims of petty revenge. Surely that would ensure her family were no longer under suspicion.

Her heart was heavy with the morning's subterfuge and scheming, but this was war and she'd do whatever it took to protect her family.

She sighed. Oh, to live in a world where honesty and integrity were the norm!

★   ★   ★

The three members of the Vannier family, Genevieve and Yves sat around the wireless set, their heads bent towards it, straining to hear each word . . .

'Before we begin, please listen to

239

some personal messages . . . ' the BBC presenter on the wireless said. 'The child's toy was left out in the rain . . . Bees are swarming at the bottom of the garden . . . I must clean the grease from my spectacles . . . The Camembert is ripe and the cider fresh . . . '

Genevieve looked at Yves. *The Camembert is ripe and the cider fresh* was the signal that the SOE would send a Lysander plane to Normandy to fetch their agents the following evening. 'They're coming for us!' she whispered almost unable to believe she and Yves would soon be home.

For the first time since the previous evening when they'd been alone in the secret room, Yves made eye contact with her and smiled.

Alexandre switched off the wireless and rose with a glass of cider in his hand, 'A toast to freedom! Vive la France!'

The others rose and clinked glasses.

'How did you do it, Oncle Alexandre?'

'I left first thing this morning and met up with the local Resistance group. They managed to get a message to London and since the conditions will be perfect, they arranged it for tomorrow.

That night, the family dined together although everyone listened out for the dogs barking. Yves seemed more relaxed — although not, Genevieve noted, with her, but certainly with her uncle.

To her relief, her aunt made her up a spare bed in Gabrielle's room and Yves slept in the secret room on his own.

That night, as she lay in bed awake, long after Gabrielle's breathing had become deep and rhythmic, she wondered if Yves was asleep. She shivered with delight as she remembered his breath on her skin, his hands caressing her. Her fingers remembered the silky-smoothness of his chest, the contours of his muscles. Then the memory of her aunt's knock on the door and Yves apologising for his unacceptable behaviour.

How that word hurt.

Tomorrow night when they flew back to England in the aircraft, he would not be able to avoid her. Lysander planes were small and they'd be sitting together on the seat in the rear of the tiny cabin throughout the flight. She would talk to him then. She suspected he would say it was because he was the circuit organiser and therefore needed to focus on his work for the SOE and Resistance, but they were both heading home and would undoubtedly be given leave before being reassigned roles in France. Until then, surely, they could talk to each other about what had happened between them.

★ ★ ★

Genevieve clutched her bag tightly to her chest and following Yves, she ran towards the Lysander aircraft which had stopped in Alexandre's field. Yves waited at the ladder on the side of the plane and held her bag while she got in. He climbed up, tossed her bag in and then handed her his rucksack which she put on her lap, out of his way. She was strapping herself in when she realised he hadn't got into the plane beside her but was outside, looking into the cabin.

'I'm sorry, Angelique,' he said. 'I'm not coming with you. There's a letter for you in my bag. And if you wouldn't mind, please could you post the other one to my parents?'

Surely she'd misheard! Why would he give up the opportunity to go home? She struggled to undo the belt but the bags were in the way and by the time she'd found the buckle, the door had closed and the plane was bumping across the grass before becoming airborne.

His letter explained that Alexandre had decided to travel to the château and find out for himself if he could help his father and Yves had offered to go with him. Now all the time the two men had spent studying maps of the Loire

Valley and discussing the terrain made sense. Genevieve had spent the day with her aunt and cousin helping with the farm chores and she'd assumed Yves was avoiding her by spending time with her uncle, but it seemed they'd been planning this without telling her.

She wanted to yell at the pilot to take her back but of course, that wasn't possible. He'd already risked his life getting to France to pick her up and they were in danger until they touched down in England. She would simply have to accept that Yves had deserted her.

★ ★ ★

Back in SOE headquarters in Baker Street, London, she was thoroughly debriefed.

Henri had sent one message since Genevieve had last seen him to say that several of the French resisters had been arrested and it was thought the circuit had been infiltrated and the members betrayed. He was on the run and promised to send a message when he could, but he'd not been heard from since.

Genevieve gave a full report about the now non-operational Tulip Circuit and its former members and she was then given a week's leave.

5

Genevieve went home to her parents' house in Greenwich. They were overjoyed to see her and that both their children were under their roof again, although they accepted it would only be for a short time. Genevieve made it clear she would go back to France as soon as SOE would send her. JP also wanted to return to France but after suffering a bout of pneumonia following his ill-treatment in prison, he was taking longer to make a full recovery than he'd expected.

Genevieve told them about Grandpère and the Germans in his château and explained how her friend Yves was helping Alexandre.

Lucienne was happy her brother had put aside his differences with their father but was desperately sad at the circumstances that had pushed Alexandre to swallow his pride. If he and Yves managed to get her papa away from the château, it would probably mean the estate would be confiscated which would hurt him deeply.

Each night when Genevieve was on her own, she re-read Yves' letter. It was plain, pragmatic, written from one operative to another. He'd avoided anything that hinted at closeness between them, let alone the night in the secret room. He appeared to have turned off the memory of the times they'd spent together, but Genevieve had been unable to do the same. She longed see him, to hear his laugh, to breath him in, feel his hands on her skin.

Why had he suddenly switched all emotion off? She bought a stamp and was about to post the letter he'd asked her to send to his mother when she had an idea. Why not deliver it in person?

Part of her thought it would probably

be a waste of time, travelling down to Dorset simply to hand a letter to a woman who might not even be there, but the other part wanted to be near anything that meant a lot to him, and perhaps to pretend for a while she was part of his world.

* * *

Genevieve checked the address on the envelope and looked through the enormous gates in front of her, along the drive that led to the mansion, rolling countryside in the distance. He'd given no hint at such wealth, having mostly spoken about his childhood in France. She walked along the drive towards two gardeners who were clipping the edges of the grass. It occurred to her that Yves' parents might not be the owners but simply employees on this grand estate.

'Can we 'elp you, Miss?' one of them asked.

'I'm looking for Mrs Leyton.'

'Keep going,' he said, pointing along the drive.

'Should I go round the back of the house?'

The man pushed his hat back and scratched his head. 'I reckon you should go to the front door.' The other man nodded his agreement.

'But where does Mrs Leyton work?' she asked.

'Work? Why bless you, Miss, she don't work! That's what she's got us for.'

'You mean Mr Leyton owns this . . . ?' she waved her hand at the immense estate.

'That's right, Miss.'

Genevieve began to wish she'd simply put the letter in the post, but it would be foolish not to carry on now, so she continued walking to the grand front entrance and climbed the steps.

When the butler opened the door, she handed in the letter and remembering Yves' real name was Mark, she said he'd asked her to deliver it. The butler thanked her and closed the door. Genevieve got to the bottom step when she heard a woman's voice calling, 'Miss! Please wait!'

It had to be Yves' mother. She was tall with the same colour hair as her son, although hers was a mass of waves, and there was something about her face which echoed Yves. 'I'm Marjorie Leyton,' she said, running down the steps, her hand extended. 'I'd like to thank you for bringing this letter. Do you know my son, Miss . . . em?'

'Lawrence, Genevieve Lawrence. And yes, I know Mark. He asked me to get the letter to you.'

'Miss Lawrence, I'd be delighted if you'd come inside and talk to me.' Without waiting for a reply, she ran back up the steps and called for the butler to bring tea and cake.

Genevieve followed her into the grand house.

A young blonde woman looked up as they entered the drawing room, her delicately arched eyebrows rising in what Genevieve thought might be annoyance.

Mrs Leyton introduced the two women. 'Miss Genevieve Lawrence,' she said waving a hand in her direction, 'Please meet Miss Lydia Ingham, a, em . . . family friend. We were just about to take tea. We'd be delighted if you'd join us.'

Lydia rose and held out a limp hand to Genevieve, then sat again and smoothed the skirt of her pink dress with manicured hands.

'You're a member of the ATS, Miss Lawrence, how exciting,' Lydia said in a bored voice.

'Miss Lawrence is a FANY, actually,' Mrs Leyton said before Genevieve could reply.

'I can never work out who's who with all those drab uniforms. Khaki's not a very flattering colour,' she said, eyeing her host warily.

'Miss Lawrence has brought word from Mark.'

At this, Lydia's eyes opened wide and

she sat up straight. 'How is he?' she asked eagerly.

'He was well the last time I saw him,' Genevieve said.

'Miss Lawrence has kindly delivered a letter from him,' Mrs Leyton said, turning the unopened envelope over in her hands.

Lydia turned away from Genevieve, watching the letter in Mrs Leyton's hands but the older woman showed no sign of opening it. Finally, Lydia checked her watch and rose, 'I'm afraid I shall have to go. I have an appointment at the hairdresser. I'll see you this evening, Mrs Leyton.' She turned to Genevieve. 'Goodbye, Miss . . .'

'Lawrence,' Genevieve said.

'Goodbye, Miss Lawrence,' Lydia said without making eye contact.

Once Lydia left, Mrs Leyton slit open the envelope and eagerly pulled out the letter which she read. She sighed. 'As expected, it doesn't tell me much but at least when he wrote it he was alive and well. He tells me you've been doing the same sort of work. I know it's secret but I wonder if you can fill in any details? He says you've both been working in France, but that's all.'

'I'm so sorry, there's not much I can tell you except your son is an exceptional man — brave, strong and committed. I'd trust him with my life. I know he's in Normandy, but other than that, I'm afraid I don't know.'

Mrs Leyton nodded sadly. 'Yes, I understand. Thank you for what you have told me and for bringing this letter. I'm very grateful, as will be my husband when he returns.' She slipped the letter back in its envelope. 'In fact, I think my husband would very much like to meet you. Would you stay the night? We have a small gathering this evening and it would be marvellous if you would join us.'

★ ★ ★

Genevieve felt out of place at the table in the huge dining room. Several of the men were in uniform but she was the only woman not in an evening gown.

'You look simply splendid,' Mrs Leyton said when Genevieve apologised. 'You're an example to all the ladies here. My guests are indebted to you and your fellow service men and women. Although none but my husband has any idea of the sort of danger you face in the line of duty.'

Mr Leyton greeted her warmly. 'You must forgive us for keeping you here. It's been so long since we've seen Mark. Your presence is a link with our son. I hope that doesn't sound foolish.'

It didn't. Although Genevieve didn't say so, she felt the same. Being in Yves' home with his parents gave her the feeling she was connected to him though she knew he was many miles away.

'Miss . . . em . . . ' Lydia Ingham caught sight of Genevieve, her eyebrows rising in surprise. 'I didn't realise you'd still be here. Shouldn't you be on duty somewhere?'

'I'm on leave. And the name is Lawrence,' Genevieve said, not wanting to spend any time with the rude girl.

'Yes, yes, of course, Miss Lawrence,' Lydia said, slipping her arm through Genevieve's. 'I wonder if you could tell me where Mark is stationed. I'd like to write, you see . . . ' she said confidentially, leaning towards Genevieve so no one else could hear. 'Before Mark left, he asked me to marry him. I needed time to think but I've made my mind up and intend to accept him. So, you see, I really need to know where he is.'

Genevieve swallowed but tried to maintain her composure. 'I'm so sorry, Miss Ingham but as I told you earlier, I don't know where he is.'

'He's a soldier, so he must be stationed somewhere!' Lydia said. 'Even I know that.'

'I'm sorry, Miss Ingham,' Genevieve said disengaging her arm. 'I'm afraid I can't help you.'

Genevieve had come to Dorset in the hope she'd feel a connection with Yves, that if she saw where he lived and the things he'd have been familiar with, it would bring his memory closer but she'd been wrong.

She'd never felt further from him.

Before he'd left, he'd asked Lydia Ingham to marry him. No wonder he'd said he'd behaved unacceptably when they'd been in the hidden room. He was in love with another woman and the Calvados had temporarily blinded him before a knock on the door had brought him back to his senses! Well, at least now, she understood.

She tried to feel angry but the truth was that in France the world of social gatherings and dinner parties such as he'd attended in Dorset before the war was a million miles away. She certainly couldn't accuse him of having led her on — if anything, it'd been she who'd pulled him to her. In the end, he'd resisted. When he came home he could marry Lydia with no reason to feel guilt.

That night, in a beautifully appointed guest bedroom in Yves' home, Genevieve stared out of the window and squeezed the heart charm between finger and thumb. Somehow she felt cheated. The only man who'd ever given her a heart had meant it only to bring luck. It had worked because despite the danger she'd faced in France, she was still alive.

As for anyone giving her a love token, that would never happen. The man she loved was out of reach because he was engaged to another. The tiny heart glinted in the moonlight, seeming to mock her. She pulled at the charm angrily trying to tug it from her watch bracelet but it held fast.

All right, let it stay, she thought. From now on hearts would only represent luck. She was no longer interested in love. If she couldn't have Yves, she didn't want anyone. She would dedicate her life to her work and she would need luck — and plenty of it. Love had no place in her life.

★ ★ ★

On her return to duty she requested she be sent out to France immediately. She wanted to join the circuit operating in Normandy in the hope she would be near her uncle and aunt and find out what had happened to her grandfather. She didn't allow herself the thought she might also see Yves. To her disappointment, it was decided that since the collapse of the Tulip Circuit she would be sent to the Loire Valley to join the newly established Dragon Circuit.

Within a few days, she had new orders and once again set off for France.

★ ★ ★

Genevieve's mouth was dry with fear but she tried to look confident. At least it was her second parachute drop over Occupied France. The new agent sitting opposite her was rigid with fright and she smiled at him encouragingly. One of the Halifax crew members led them to the opening in the fuselage and they clipped on their static lines watching the dark shadows on the ground hundreds of feet below. The agent's face was pale. She tapped him on the arm to attract his attention. 'See you on the ground,' she said.

The red light on the bulkhead switched to green and Genevieve dropped through the hole in the fuselage into the night sky, her static line pulling open the canopy.

For a second, she hung in the darkness, a chilly wind whipping at her face and then, as she began to float gently downwards she could see the torches below and hoped they belonged to members of the Dragon Circuit waiting for her, and not a German ambush.

She rolled as she landed and as she was gathering up her parachute, two men carrying automatic weapons ran towards her.

'Angelique!' one of them said in a

voice she recognised. It was Henri. She threw her arms about his neck and hugged him tightly.

Dozens of parachutes wafted down to the waiting men and the packages suspended beneath them were quickly gathered and packed into a waiting van, with the new agent and Genevieve.

There was another pleasant surprise for her — the man in the driving seat with the Gauloises cigarette clamped between his lips turned to her and smiled. It was Marcel Pélissier.

The Dragon Circuit headquarters was in a room at the back of a shoe factory on the edge of town. The van and a car pulled through large wooden gates into the factory yard, and immediately Pierre, the leader of the circuit, began to direct the unloading and storage of the crates.

Once everything was hidden, Genevieve was introduced to Pierre. Immediately, she knew this was a man with whom she could work. He was tall and athletic with sandy hair and inspired confidence in others with his calm, common sense and geniality. She detected a steely determination in him that matched her own. The new agent who'd been so afraid to jump out of the Halifax bomber was called Paul, an explosives expert who, though still nervous, seemed much more at ease now he was on terra firma.

During the following few weeks, under Pierre's experienced eye, the members of the Dragon Circuit came to rely on each other and form a formidable force which had taken Churchill's order to the SOE to 'Set Europe ablaze!' to heart.

Liaising with London via Henri's wireless set, attacks on factories which had been pressed to work for the Germans and other installations important to the enemy, had been bombed or set on fire at the same time as RAF bombers passed overhead. It was an obvious assumption to make, that the explosions and fires had been caused by the bombers but in fact, aerial bombardment could not hit targets with as much accuracy as people on the ground who knew exactly where to place their explosives to cause maximum damage. Pierre kept to a small number of members — the more members, the more likelihood of betrayal, Genevieve knew, so Pierre had been wise. Everyone could be trusted.

For the moment anyway.

Each evening, they tuned in to the BBC for the personal messages. They were waiting to hear the coded message telling them to expect more guns if the weather was fine. Genevieve was also listening for news of her grandfather. In Yves' letter to her, he'd said that if he and her uncle managed to get her grandfather free, they'd try to send a message via the BBC.

'Before we begin, please listen to some personal messages . . . ' the BBC presenter on the wireless said, 'Brother George has an earache . . . The water is cool but quite refreshing . . . The pink pig is muddy . . . Grand-père is sipping cider . . . '

Genevieve gasped. That was the code to tell her Oncle Alexandre and Yves had got Grand-père away from the château.

'Shh!' said Pierre, waiting for his message. 'A walk in the park is just what I need . . . '

That was the code he was waiting for. Genevieve was pleased but nothing could eclipse her delight at knowing her grandfather had been rescued and sipping cider safely at Oncle Alexandre's farm.

★ ★ ★

Marcel had contacts among the railway workers, many of whom were members of the Resistance. They'd shown Genevieve and the others how to sabotage trains in a way which was both effective and undetectable. A handful of grit in the axles allowed a train to move from the sidings, only to seize up several miles along the track, blocking lines and disrupting the railway system. Pierre arranged for several large railway cranes used for removing obstacles from lines to be damaged, devastating deliveries of goods and troops.

After one such successful operation, Genevieve was cycling home, keeping her distance from Pierre who was ahead, and knowing that Henri was following her at a discreet distance, when she thought she saw someone she recognised. She slowed down and dismounted, crouching down to look at her bicycle chain as if there was a problem. Looking up as Henri passed her with an anxious expression, she flashed him a brief smile to show all was well, and he carried on.

Genevieve wheeled the bicycle to the Café Les Pêcheurs. Leaning it outside, she entered. The air was thick with cigarette smoke and there was a loud hum of conversation but a quick scan didn't reveal any German uniforms. That didn't mean there weren't any plain clothes officers present, so she walked to the counter and waited for the proprietor to finish pouring drinks, not looking at the person she'd thought she'd recognised. It was definitely her — Nathalie, or as Genevieve reminded herself, Estelle, her code name.

Most of the tables were taken, so Genevieve walked to Nathalie's table. 'Bonsoir Mademoiselle, is this seat taken?'

Nathalie looked up and after a moment's shock, composed her face as if she'd never seen Genevieve before.

'No, please take it,' she said in the tone of someone who wasn't happy about her space being invaded — but beneath the table, she gripped Genevieve's hand for a few seconds, to show her delight. To an observer, it would have appeared that two young strangers who had to share a table were making the best of things by carrying on a stilted, desultory conversation. However, within a short space of time, the two girls had swapped information before parting.

★ ★ ★

'Yves arrested?' Marcel stared at Genevieve, his mouth open in shock.

'Are you sure, Angelique?' Henri asked.

'Yes. My friend is part of the Monarch Circuit and she said the group Yves joined near Caen was ambushed while they were waiting for a drop. They were all taken to Fresnes Prison. We've got to do something!' she said looking at Pierre.

'We don't have the manpower to break anyone out of prison,' Pierre said. 'But we can find out more and ask for help from London. We'd need to know how many there are in prison.'

'I'll find out,' Marcel said, lighting a Gauloises and drawing on it deeply.

It was decided Marcel and Genevieve should go by train to Fresnes, posing as a married couple. Once there, Marcel would make enquiries and see if he could contact local resisters who might help. It was going to be much harder to get anyone out of Fresnes with its tight security, than it had been to bribe a guard and free JP.

Genevieve waited for Marcel in a nearby café, nervously moving her heart charm between finger and thumb. She tried to appear calm so as not to attract attention but as soon as Marcel entered the café, she could tell he had bad news.

'We're too late,' he whispered. 'He's gone.'

'Gone where?' Genevieve whispered urgently.

'To a German concentration camp.'

★ ★ ★

Genevieve cried that night and for many of the following nights. Silent tears slid down her cheeks and such a terrible longing gripped her. The pain was so great it was physical, and each morning she woke from broken, nightmare-filled sleep with puffy, dark eyes and pale skin. It had been weeks since she'd heard about Yves being transferred to a concentration camp and now, winter was approaching. She knew conditions would be dire.

'If you're sick, Angelique, we should send you back to London,' Pierre said in his usual pragmatic way.

'I'm fine, I've had trouble sleeping lately.'

Henri looked at her over the top of his glasses, 'You'd better be fine,' he said. 'We've just got new orders from London. It's going to be big. A consignment of Panzer tanks is being transported to Calais on a train crossing the bridge on Tuesday. Our orders are to blow up the bridge, stop the delivery, destroy as many tanks as possible.'

After that, there'd been no time for Genevieve to dwell on Yves' fate. There could be no delay. They must be ready to blow up the bridge on Tuesday whatever the cost.

Marcel returned from his meeting with a local Resistance group with bad news. The roadblocks had been increased so getting to the bridge was going to be almost impossible. He'd got through with a load of plastic explosives and guns hidden in his van but on his return, he saw long queues of people and vehicles being thoroughly searched.

'We need detonators, and hand grenades,' he said. 'I'll go in again. Perhaps first thing in the morning. Security might not be so tight tomorrow.'

Pierre rubbed his chin. 'We'll have to think of another way. If you're caught the Germans will know there's to be an attack. This must not fail.'

'I'll take them through the checkpoint,' said Genevieve immediately.

'That's very brave, old girl,' said Henri, 'but even you and your famous legs aren't going to take all those guards' minds off their work while you stroll through with a load of detonators in your basket.'

'You just watch me!' said Genevieve.

6

It was time to leave. Already the nuns had been subject to a search of their convent by the Germans. How long before they looked more thoroughly and discovered the concealed entrance to the crypt? Yves was certain he wouldn't be so lucky the next time they came. Mother Superior and her nuns had been wonderful, but now he'd recovered, he owed it to them to go — now.

He looked around the dusty vault which had been his home for the last few weeks. Most of it had passed in a haze of delirious dreams.

He could recall being interrogated at Fresnes Prison after the German ambush at the dropping zone. The agents had been seized as well as the weapons. It had been a disaster.

Fresnes Prison was something Yves would have liked to have forgotten but the maltreatment regularly visited him in his nightmares. He'd lost track of the weeks he'd been locked up but he hadn't cracked. He'd told the Germans nothing. Eventually, he and another member of the circuit, Ralph, had been loaded onto a train which the guard said was bound for a concentration camp in Germany.

Not far from the French border, somewhere near Nancy, there was a tremendous explosion. Wheels screeched and the engine juddered and swayed as it derailed. It slithered and rolled down the steep embankment, dragging the carriages behind it. Chains secured the prisoners' handcuffs to a metal ring, anchored in the wall of the carriage and prevented them being hurled down the length of the coach like the guards. Their wrists were bruised and cut and they were lacerated by broken glass but when they finally came to a standstill, Ralph and Yves were the only ones in the carriage still alive. The force of the crash had splintered the walls of the carriage and though still bound by the handcuffs, they pulled the rings free and drag themselves out from the carnage.

'Hands up!' A masked man shouted in French, pointing an automatic weapon at them.

'Don't shoot!' Yves pleaded, and at the sight of the handcuffs and the sound of his French accent, the masked man lowered his gun.

The members of the French Resistance who'd targeted the train helped Yves and Ralph out of the wreckage and to a nearby thicket. Bullets whizzed past as German soldiers in the last carriage of the train found their weapons and fired.

Even now, weeks later, Yves woke at night remembering Ralph's scream as the impact of a bullet propelled him forward and threw him to the ground. Wanting to help his friend, Yves hesitated, but the hands holding him kept him moving. Then something hit the side of his head, causing flashes of blinding light . . . and then nothing

. . . until he woke bathed in sweat, Angelique wiping his forehead with a cool cloth and whispering calming words to soothe him.

Sometime later, he woke again with his mind clear and his body no longer burning up with fever. He learned that a bullet had skimmed his head, knocking him out and ripping through his skin. That wound and the many lacerations from the broken glass had become infected. The resisters had managed to get him to the convent where he'd lain delirious and near death.

Once his fever had broken, he was puzzled to find Angelique gone, and in her place a succession of nuns brought him food and water.

In despair, he realised it had been the nuns with their black veils leaning over him all along, his delirious brain interpreting it as Angelique's sleek, dark hair falling over her face. She hadn't been there at all.

He had almost given up then.

During one of Mother Superior's visits, she'd said he'd called out repeatedly for Angelique and asked him if she was his wife or sweetheart.

He'd shaken his head sadly.

'Would it help to talk about it?'

What could he say? He couldn't tell her how they'd met, nor how they'd worked together because that was classified information.

Mother Superior, seeing his reluctance, asked, 'This girl . . . she is married?' He shook his head. 'Pledged to another?'

'I believe so.'

'You believe so? You don't know for sure?'

Yves told her about the heart-shaped charm and how she'd hesitated when he'd asked if someone special had given it to her.

Mother Superior frowned. 'But did she actually say she was committed to another?'

'No, but if she didn't have someone, wouldn't she have said so?'

'She may have a sweetheart somewhere, but to jump to conclusions like that because the girl hesitated . . .' She didn't finish the sentence but it was obvious she doubted Yves' reasoning.

He had plenty of time on his own to think and wondered if he'd judged Angelique unfairly. His only experience of women had been Lydia Ingham and she'd proved to be scheming and selfish. He knew she was a convincing liar, always with a ready excuse. But Angelique . . . she'd never given him reason to doubt her, so why hadn't he simply waited until she'd explained? Had he been afraid she had someone special because deep down he knew he was falling for her? Or had he dreaded the thought she might lie to him like Lydia had? He wouldn't have been able to bear that.

'I'm sure you'll get over her soon. When you're back in England, everything will look very different,' Mother Superior said.

You'll get over her soon. That wasn't

possible. He'd thought of nothing but Angelique since his fever had broken. She was the first thought to enter his head when he woke and the last to drift away as he went to sleep at night. Memories of them lying entwined in the secret room at her uncle's house filled him with joy and then despair when he remembered how he'd pushed her away, jealous at the thought of her with someone else but afraid to let her into his life.

Now, he had to see her. He'd never be at peace unless he saw her again and found out if she had someone waiting for her. That was when he decided he wouldn't go home to England until he'd found Angelique.

Easier said than done since he had no idea where she was. If London had sent her back to France they could have placed her anywhere. It was most likely though, that they'd send her back to where Tulip Circuit had operated, in an area she knew well. If that was so, then Yves could think of one man who'd know — Marcel Pélissier.

Yves left the convent that evening, dressed in a smart suit Mother Superior had given him. As he left, she took his hand and pressed some money and a small metal disc into his palm.

'This may come in handy,' she said. 'In that suit, you have the look of a plain clothes Gestapo officer. I'm sorry I could not get you the proper identification papers, but you may be able to bluff your way through, at least until you contact someone to help you.'

He looked at the warrant disc in the palm of his hand, Geheime Staatspolizei stamped on one side. There were strict rules governing the identity of Gestapo field personnel and when asked for identification, an operative was required only to present his warrant disc which identified him as Gestapo without revealing personal identity.

Yves slipped it in his pocket. The nuns had recently shaved his blonde hair to match the area around his

wound and he looked every inch a
Gestapo agent.

* * *

The German soldier's eyes flickered
from Yves' face to the warrant disc he
nonchalantly moved over in the palm of
his hand.

'Pass,' the guard said, without further
delay and Yves kept his pace deliberately slow as he walked away from the
checkpoint. To appear to be in a hurry
would draw unwanted attention.

Marcel lived with his wife and
children in the country but when he
was in town, he stayed with his uncle,
so Yves thought he'd try there first. As
he scanned the faces around him, ever
on the lookout for danger, he stopped
so abruptly that a man ploughed into
the back of him.

Yves didn't apologise. He couldn't
speak. Nor could he take his eyes off a
girl across the street.

Angelique.

278

She was about to join the queue to go through the checkpoint he'd just come through. A sandy-haired man was with her, his arm protectively around her shoulders and Yves' stomach lurched with jealousy. *It's an act!* He told himself. Hadn't he and Angelique often walked along the streets hand in hand as if they were sweethearts in order to avoid closer inspection by the German authorities? Whoever the man was, he was almost certainly an SOE agent or member of the local Resistance and he and Angelique were pretending to be sweethearts in the same way. Except one of the man's hands was on Angelique's shoulder and the other resting on her hands — which were placed protectively on her heavily pregnant belly.

Yves forced himself to keep walking. Could it be possible Angelique really was pregnant and the sandy-haired man wasn't playing a part to fool the Germans?

Walk! Find Marcel. He'll know.

With his short hair, gaunt face and thin frame after the hardship and starvation in prison, Yves appeared very different from the man he'd been the last time Marcel's uncle had seen him.

'Yes?' Marcel's uncle said when he opened the door slightly, his eyes narrow with suspicion.

'Bonjour Monsieur Pélissier, please can you tell me where Marcel is.'

'Who wants to know?'

Yves introduced himself and suspicion changed to doubt as Marcel's uncle scrutinised Yves' face, then finally to surprise as he recognised him. The door opened and Monsieur Pélissier grabbed his shoulder and pulled him into the house.

Over coffee, he explained there was a big operation in progress which should result in the destruction of a train transporting Panzer tanks to the coast. The railway bridge was to be blown up and the train and its cargo would be prevented from reaching their destination.

'Where's Marcel now?' Yves asked.

'I'm not sure but I know where he'll be later. The explosion should take place in about . . . ' He checked his watch. 'Fifty minutes. If all goes well, there'll be soldiers and roadblocks for miles around, so Marcel and the others aren't going to try to get away. They'll stay for a few days in a small hotel in town, until things quieten down.

'And Angelique?' Yves asked nonchalantly, 'Will she be there?'

'The girl?' Marcel's uncle shrugged, 'No idea. Where are you staying tonight?'

Yves hadn't decided. He'd hoped to find Marcel and see if he could get him to a safe house.

'If I were you,' Marcel's uncle said, 'I'd find somewhere quickly. Once that bridge goes up, you'd best be off the streets. The Boches are going to be crawling all over town.'

Yves thanked him and made his way

to the address he'd been given — Hotel Auberrac in a small alley off the Rue du Pont.

Despite Monsieur Pélissier's prediction about the timing of the explosion, it went off early. The first blast rattled the windows of the shops Yves was walking past and it was followed by several other explosions and the high-pitched squeal of metal against metal.

Within minutes, sirens rang out and soldiers were on the streets. Yves turned off the main road, keeping to the quieter side streets, a circuitous route towards Rue du Pont.

When he finally found the hotel, he knew why Marcel had chosen it: a rundown building with a faded sign out of the way at the end of a narrow, cobbled alley. Yves quietly entered and waited at the desk for the owner who was on the telephone in the office.

Yves was about to ring the bell for attention when he heard the man say ' . . . suspicious . . . they arrived today. Three of them . . . '

Yves stepped to one side so the man wouldn't see him if he looked up.

'I went in his room and looked in his bag . . . something that looked like a detonator . . . yes, they're booked for a week . . . one woman and two men. The woman's pregnant . . . they're upstairs now. You'll send someone? And you'll compensate me? After all, if you take away my guests I'll be out of pocket . . . Hello? Hello?'

Yves' first thought was to run upstairs and find Marcel, Angelique and the other man, but he didn't know which rooms they were in. At one time, he'd have threatened the wretched hotel owner, but he hadn't regained his strength after being in prison. He'd have to use his wits.

Yves drew himself up to full height and slammed his hand down on the bell. Taking the warrant disc from his pocket, Yves held it out for the man to see. 'I understand you have guests we may be interested in,' Yves said trying to give his French a German accent.

'I only just called,' he looked from Yves haughty expression to the telephone and back again.

'We've had your hotel under surveillance for some time. I was not far away,' Yves said. 'Now, where are these suspicious people?'

The proprietor jerked his thumb upwards. 'Second floor. The woman's in number twelve at the top of the stairs, the two men are in fourteen.'

'Is there a rear entrance?' Yves asked.

'Yes, through there.' The man pointed down a corridor to a door.

'Is it locked?'

The man shook his head. 'About my compensation, Monsieur . . . ?' he said.

Yves ignored him. 'Are there any other members of staff on the premises?'

'No, just me.'

'Good. Do you have a cellar?' The man nodded. 'Then I suggest you go down there, lock the door and wait until the shooting stops.'

'Sh . . . shooting?'

'The people upstairs are dangerous.

They must be taken — dead or alive.'

The man hurried away, and as soon as he'd gone, Yves locked the main doors and took the stairs two at a time to the second floor. He tapped on the door of room twelve, insistent but not loudly.

'Who is it?' Angelique was on the other side, waiting for a password that he didn't know.

'It's Yves!' he said as loudly as he dared, hoping she'd recognise his voice. 'Open up!'

He could hear whispering from behind the door. They would be waiting with guns drawn because he hadn't given the correct password but hopefully, he'd planted enough doubt in their mind that they wouldn't shoot first. The door opened a crack and an eye observed him for a few seconds.

'You're in danger!' Yves said, 'Angelique, Marcel, if you're in there, the hotel owner has called the Gestapo! We've got to get out — now!'

The door opened wide, revealing a

tall, sandy-haired man, Marcel, and Angelique.

Yves led the way downstairs and into a small yard at the back. It was littered with discarded items and Pierre dragged an old table next to the wall and held it stable. One by one, they climbed on and scrambled onto the top of the wall, then held out their hands to haul Pierre up with them. They jumped down, looking right and left.

'Split up,' Pierre said, 'Marcel, take our friend. Angelique, with me. We'll meet at the factory.'

'But you said it was too dangerous to go to any of our usual places . . . ' Angelique said.

Pierre shrugged, 'We don't have any choice. We've got to get off the streets. Now run!'

'Mon ami! It is so good to see you!' Marcel said as he began to run in the opposite direction to Pierre and Angelique, 'Come, follow me.'

Marcel was familiar with the town and led Yves through alleys and across back gardens. They arrived at the shoe factory before Angelique and Pierre. Yves was out of breath and his legs trembling with the effort of keeping up with Marcel, although he tried to conceal his weakness.

'From the look of things you've had a hard time,' said Marcel, when they were in the room at the back of the workshop. 'We came looking for you in Fresnes when we heard you'd been arrested but we were too late . . . now against all odds, here you are, thinner and uglier than ever!'

At a sound from outside, Marcel seized his pistol and leapt to his feet aiming at the door.

'It's us!' Pierre said. As he entered, he nodded at Marcel. 'Come with me, mon ami. We need to find out what's going on and search for somewhere safe to stay.'

'What about me? What shall I do?' Yves asked.

'Wait here. Marcel and I will be back soon.'

'Where's Angelique?' Yves asked.

'She's . . . ' Pierre looked over his shoulder, 'dressing,' he said, then left.

'I'll be back soon, mon ami,' Marcel said, slapping Yves on the back and following Pierre.

Angelique appeared at the door holding a large wicker basket. She locked the door, then turned to smile at Yves, 'Thank you so much for the warning back at the hotel. What a surprise to see you! But you always were full of surprises.'

'And you too are full of surprises,' he said scathingly, 'I admit, I hadn't expected to see you in that condition.' He nodded at her belly.

'Oh this,' she said, placing the basket on the table. 'It was a masterstroke.'

He stared as he saw she was now wearing a shirt and trousers belted tightly on a small waist.

'Wait . . . ' she said, her smile slipping to a frown, 'you really believed I was pregnant?'

'I . . . I . . . well, it looked like it . . . '

She picked the basket up and tipped out a leather harness. It was a wicker basket such as one might carry to market although the handle had been removed. 'I carried a load of detonators, hand grenades and plastic explosive through the checkpoint,' she said demonstrating how she'd strapped the basket to her body with the harness. 'With a coat on, it looked like I was pregnant. Thankfully, none of the soldiers investigated further.'

'Ingenious,' said Yves. 'You had me fooled.'

'I suppose you thought what would one expect from a woman who'd thrown herself at me?'

'Angelique! I didn't say that!'

'You didn't have to — your expression told me exactly how you felt! That time with you at my uncle's was the first time I'd been with a man. And it will be the last. Since then, I've had no time for anything other than working to free France. If my methods upset your sensibilities, too bad!'

'No, Angelique! Truly, I wasn't judging. It was just a lot to take in. I've nothing but admiration for you and what you've done here.'

She paused as if mulling over his words. Finally, she spoke more gently. 'You know we came for you at Fresnes, don't you?'

'Marcel told me.' He told her about his escape.

'I'm so sorry, Yves. I can see you've been badly treated — you're much thinner than you used to be. But don't worry, Pierre will get Henri to send a message to London to let them know you're safe. You'll be back in Dorset before you know it.' She paused, 'And this time, it'll be me seeing you off.' Her voice was bitter.

'I'm sorry. I had to leave you like that.'

'No, you didn't. I'm grateful for what you did for my family but I could've helped. I thought we were partners. Apparently not.'

'Your uncle expressly asked me not to

290

involve you. He said your grandfather would be more worried about you than himself and it would make things harder. Alexandre was right.'

Despite her indignation, she suspected he had a point. 'Is he well? Where is he now?'

'He'd been badly treated but he was improving the last time I saw him. He's renting a cottage near your uncle's farm.'

'That's such good news. I have good news for you. From Lydia . . . '

7

Genevieve kept her hands in her lap, repeatedly moving the heart charm on her watch between finger and thumb. What she longed to do was to stroke Yves' gaunt face, to hold his hand, to touch this man who she'd missed so much, but she dared not. He'd helped her uncle rescue Grand-père and he'd saved her life. And now, she had a way of pleasing him — to tell him that Lydia had accepted his marriage proposal.

'I have a message for you from Lydia.'

'Lydia?' he said, frowning as if trying to remember, 'which circuit?'

'It's not a code name,' she said. 'It's her real name. Lydia Ingham. From Dorset.'

When he finally spoke, his voice was quiet, 'How do you know Lydia?'

'I met her at your parents' house.'

'What were you doing there?'

'You asked me to make sure your mother got your letter. So I took it in person.'

'What was Lydia doing there?'

'Drinking tea and eating cake.'

Yves was silent. His dark-rimmed eyes wide open with shock. 'You said you had good news about Lydia?' he asked finally.

'Yes, she wanted me to tell you she accepts your proposal of marriage.'

She hadn't expected him to burst out laughing and it made her jump. It wasn't joyous laughter, either, but bitter and harsh.

'So, she finished with the farmer . . . or perhaps not. It'd be just like Lydia to lead him on in case I don't make it home. She's a calculating woman.'

'So it isn't welcome news?' Genevieve asked.

'It's completely irrelevant. I admit at one time when I was younger and more gullible, I'd have been elated. But now? I really don't care. I had a lucky escape from that scheming woman.'

So he didn't love Lydia!

'It looks like we've all had some lucky escapes,' Genevieve said, looking down at the heart charm.

Was there still a chance for them? Had her silver heart really brought them both good luck?

He followed the direction of her gaze.

'Once, I asked you if someone special had given you that charm,' he said. 'But I don't think I waited for an answer . . . '

'Yes, a very special man gave me this. Sonny Rayment. A pilot in the RAF. He gave it to me for my birthday.'

'I see.'

'No, you don't. The reason I hesitated when you asked before was because Sonny is a special man, kind and thoughtful. For a while, I thought Sonny might be interested in me but I was wrong. He and my friend Ellie were made for each other. I'm not sure what happened but they parted. With any luck, they'll have both come to their senses by now and got back together, but who knows? Who even knows if either of them is still alive?'

'So, you and he . . . weren't . . . '

'No, Sonny and I were never sweethearts. His mother gave him a heart-shaped locket for luck and he always associated hearts with good luck. That's why he gave me this . . . ' She held it up for him to see. 'I rub it between my finger and thumb and wish good luck for people. It seemed to have worked for you.' She smiled.

'You touched the charm and thought of me?'

He looked at her in wonder, but before she could answer him, Pierre and Marcel returned.

'We're staying here tonight. Everywhere's teeming with soldiers, but tomorrow at first light, we're heading out of town. Henri's found a place for us,' Marcel said.

There was no more opportunity for Yves and Genevieve to talk that night. Marcel and Pierre had brought back some cheese, bread and wine and they ate together by candlelight, then dozed where they sat until dawn.

Genevieve thought about the conversation she'd had with Yves earlier. She wanted to ask him why he'd turned away from her that night at her uncle's. Earlier, he'd told her how Lydia had refused his proposal in favour of someone she thought was wealthier than Yves. He said he'd been heartbroken but it hadn't taken him long to realise he was better off without her. So, although Genevieve had assumed it was loyalty to Lydia that had made him reject her, that didn't appear to be the case. Could it have been because he thought the charm meant she had someone special at home?

If only they could have finished their conversation!

★　★　★

The next morning, Henri arrived at the shoe factory and greeted Yves warmly, holding him at arm's length and shaking his head in disbelief at the bony frame and thin face.

'I've sent a message to London to tell them you're safe,' he said. 'On my next sched, I hope to hear how they're going to get you out of here. You need feeding up and time to recuperate.'

They sipped wine as they waited for Henri to set up his wireless and to tap his Morse Code key to let London know he was on air and about to transmit. He sent his report and then, with earphones on, he carefully transcribed the message he received. When he signed off, he peered at the paper gloomily.

'What's wrong?' Pierre asked.

'London's had a warning from another circuit, that the Gestapo know all about the Dragon Circuit and they're watching most of our safe houses.'

'That can't be true!' said Genevieve.

'I'm afraid it is. They obviously don't know about this place — yet — but if we return to any of our usual safe houses, we're likely to be arrested. We've orders to go south. We'll head over the Pyrenees to Spain.'

Marcel looked at Yves doubtfully. 'We need a plane to take Yves. He's not going to be able to make it that far. He couldn't keep up with me when we came here last night.'

'Then leave me,' said Yves. 'I don't want to be the cause of anyone being arrested . . . or worse.'

'No!' said Genevieve. 'I've an idea. You all head south. Yves and I will go north to my uncle's farm. He has contacts and should be able to arrange for a Lysander to pick Yves up.'

Pierre scratched his head. 'I don't like it, Angelique. You're part of my circuit and I want to see you safely out of France.'

'There's no choice, Pierre. You, Marcel, Henri and the other resisters will stand a better chance if you all go separately and make your way to the Pyrenees. I'll pretend to be pregnant, travelling with my husband to Caen for hospital treatment. Once Yves and I get to my uncle's, we'll be fine.

Pierre sighed and nodded.

'I'll send a message to inform London of our plans,' said Henri, 'and ask them to lay on a Lysander to pick you and Yves up from Normandy.'

Once Henri had sent his message to London and packed away his wireless, there was no reason to delay. They embraced each other warmly knowing the dangers they were all facing. The journey through France and across the Pyrenees would be fraught with hazards and the chance of all the men reaching Spain safely was small.

Likewise, travelling by train to Caen was also likely to be hazardous with all the checks and inspections, especially after the successful destruction of the railway bridge. Unfortunately, the explosives had gone off prematurely before the train carrying the load of Panzer tanks had arrived, although it had stopped their passage to the coast where the German army desperately needed them.

Genevieve strapped the basket back around her middle and placed two guns wrapped in cloth inside, with ammunition. Travelling as Monsieur and Madame Christophe on their way to see a specialist in Caen, they boarded the train.

How lovely it was to have Yves' arm around her shoulders and his hand holding hers. His obvious adoration was all an act, she knew, but he was so convincing that it was tempting to believe it and she closed her eyes, pretending it was real.

'Not long now, by the size of you,' the woman sitting opposite Genevieve said, nodding at her bump, 'It looks like you're carrying a boy to me.'

Genevieve smiled, yawned and pretended to fall asleep on Yves' shoulder, afraid of the woman's observations. She knew nothing about having a baby — suppose she should give herself away?

As the train pulled into the station, Yves helped her on to the platform and with his arm protectively around her, he led her outside and found a farmer who was travelling towards the coast in his lorry to give them a lift. When they asked to be dropped off in a small village, he let them out and drove off, keen to get home.

There were still a few miles to go to Alexandre's farm but Yves didn't want anyone to know their destination, especially after the black marketeer had reported their arrival the last time they'd been there. He planned to arrive at the farmhouse across the fields, hopefully without being seen.

As they walked through the narrow country lanes, Genevieve kept an anxious eye on Yves. His face was white and she knew he was struggling to keep up with her. She fought back tears, remembering how strong he'd once been but now he was painfully thin, his wrists still bore faint bruising from the handcuffs and there was a livid scar above his ear. They will heal, she told herself, his hair will grow and cover the scar and his bruises will fade in time.

'Tell me, Madame Christophe,' Yves said, recovering his breath, 'Are you and our unborn son doing well?'

They both laughed at the certainty with which the woman on the train had predicted Genevieve's 'baby's' gender. She slowed her pace so he could keep up. It would mean they'd take slightly longer to get to her uncle's, but so what? She was enjoying being with Yves.

'Yesterday, we didn't finish our conversation,' he said, staring ahead. 'You may not want to talk about what happened that night at your uncle's, but I think I owe you an explanation.' He paused, pushed his fringe back and took a deep breath. 'I suppose it all started with Lydia. She hurt me deeply. I trusted her and believed she loved me but she was more interested in finding a rich husband than a soulmate. In my naivety, I assumed all women were the same, so I was happy to come to France

and to exist in a man's
sabotage and spying. The la
needed in the circuit was
— but I fell in love with
moment I laid eyes on you!

'Not that I admitted it to myse
denied my feelings for you and
myself I was outraged London
exposed a woman to such risk and
you'd endanger the entire circuit.
course, I was wrong. You demonstrat
your competence and I came to admi
your courage and skills. It was as Hen
said — you have a fearless heart.

'When I first asked you about the
silver charm, I dreaded finding out you
had someone waiting in England.
Nevertheless, that night at your uncle's,
I was so intoxicated with you that I
convinced myself you wanted me. It
wasn't until the knock on the door that
I came to my senses. I was angry with
myself for my lack of self-control — and
angry with you because I thought you'd
led me on when you had a sweetheart.

'Now I find you didn't have anyone

all and if I hadn't been so stupid, we ght . . . well, things might've been fferent.'

They walked on in silence.

'Angelique, I've just poured out my heart to you and admitted my foolishness. Please say something . . . even if it's only to shout at me or to tell me you don't care!'

She stopped and when he saw she was crying, he put his arms around her.

'Yves! If only I'd known! I fell in love with you too, but I thought you weren't interested in me. Yet even so, I secretly hoped one day you'd want me. That was, until Lydia said you'd proposed to her — and then I thought my heart would break.'

'We've wasted so much time,' he said, resting his forehead on hers, 'Do you think we'll get another chance?'

'I don't know. We're lucky to be alive after working in France for so long. I couldn't bear it if our luck ran out before we had a chance to be together — at least for a while.'

Yves cupped her face in his hands and kissed her forehead, tenderly wiping her tears away with his thumbs, then touched his lips to hers. She pulled him close and kissed him gently, and he held her tightly as if, even for the briefest time, their love could protect them from the horrors of the war that surrounded them.

'After my fever broke and I knew I loved you, I dared not dream you'd want me too. Now I don't ever want to let you out of my sight. I want to spend the rest of my life with you, Angelique, no matter how long or short that might be,' Yves said, stroking her hair.

*　*　*

'Genevieve! Ma petite!' Denise held up her hands although whether in shock at seeing her niece on the doorstep or in horror because of her large belly, Genevieve couldn't tell.

'Come in, come in!' Denise ushered them inside the house and took them into the kitchen where her husband, daughter and father-in-law were at the table. When they saw Genevieve and Yves, they rose and gathered around the pair.

'Is this your doing?' Grand-père asked Yves, pointing at Genevieve's bump in outrage.

'Grand-père! This is just a disguise!' Genevieve said, aware of their surprised glances. 'It made it easier for us to travel without attracting attention.' She removed the basket and displayed the two guns and ammunition she'd concealed inside.

Grand-père told her how Yves and Alexandre had snatched him from under the Germans' noses. 'I expect the Boches will have drunk all the wine in the cellars and ruined the château but at least I'm free, thanks to your fine young man and my son.'

'After we've eaten, I'll see what can be done about arranging passage out of France for you two,' Alexandre said, 'You both deserve a rest — and Yves needs fattening up.'

After the meal, Grand-père put his coat on and turned to Yves. 'Come along young man, I have a spare bed in my cottage.'

Genevieve's heart sank. After their earlier kiss she longed to spend the night alone with Yves, but Grand-père's sense of propriety was going to spoil it. It was impossible to know if London would want her home as well as Yves. If not, she'd have to wait for orders, perhaps join the closest circuit. How long before she saw Yves again?

'No!' said Denise to her father-in-law, 'It's better, Beau-papa, if Yves stays here with us. We have the hidden room. If anyone comes to your cottage in the middle of the night, Beau-papa, where are you going to hide Yves?'

'I suppose you have a point,' said Grand-père.

'Our priority is your grand-daughter and her friend's safety,' Denise added.

Genevieve had no idea if her aunt suspected how she felt about Yves or if she simply had safety in mind but she was grateful to be allowed one night alone with Yves.

'At least this time, you've both eaten a meal,' Denise said, 'and we don't have an unwanted guard downstairs. So hopefully we should have a peaceful night.' She handed Genevieve a candle and after closing the door, pulled the chest of drawers back into position, hiding the entrance.

Now they were alone, Genevieve's courage failed her. She'd yearned for Yves and imagined what might have happened if they hadn't been disturbed last time. Now she didn't know what to do.

'Are you going to stand there staring at that candle until it goes out?' Yves asked, coming behind her and placing his hands on her shoulders.

'I suddenly feel very shy,' she said.

'The girl with the fearless heart who carries guns through checkpoints under the noses of the Germans and who helped blow up railway lines, telephone exchanges and factories is afraid?'

'I didn't say I was afraid.'

'Does this help?' He leaned over her shoulder and blew out the candle.

'Now I can't see anything,' she said.

'Good. Now you can't see how afraid *I* am.'

She could hear the laughter in his voice.

'Angelique, we don't have to do anything. It's enough to have you next to me all night and to wake up with you in the morning,' he whispered. Still behind her, he enfolded her in his arms and rested his cheek on the top of her head.

She placed her hands over his, holding his arms around her body and leaned back against him. His warmth radiated through her dress and in the darkness the feeling of security in his encircling arms banished all thoughts of the outside world.

'If these were normal times,' Yves whispered, 'we could do things at a slow pace. I'd take you out for dinner in a restaurant and dance with you until the early hours. It'd give us time to get to know each other . . . and then we might find ourselves together, like this . . . '

She turned to face him. 'Well, we haven't been to a restaurant but we have eaten dinner and now there's nothing stopping us dancing.'

'There's no music.'

'Yes, there is,' she said. 'Listen . . . '

They held each other tightly in the silent darkness and moved slowly to a rhythm that neither could hear, but both recognised.

'You said if we had more time together it would give us a chance to get to know each other,' Genevieve said, 'but the truth is, I don't know anyone as well as I know you. I trust you with my life. And time is a luxury we may not have . . . '

'What are you saying, Angelique?'

'I'm not saying anything,' she said undoing her dress and allowing it to slip to the floor. Taking his hand, she led him to the bed. She undid his shirt buttons and slipped her hand inside, feeling the silky smoothness of his skin. 'The last time we were here, you did this to me . . . ' She traced her fingertip around his mouth. 'And then you did this . . . ' She kissed his lips. 'Then you kissed me here . . . ' She placed his hand above her breast. 'And now, it's up to you. You're the man who makes the plans.'

'I think under the circumstances there's only one course of action . . . ' She gasped with pleasure as his lips found the place she'd indicated — then carried on exploring her body.

*   *   *

They awoke in the morning, their bodies entwined. He smiled at her when she opened her eyes. 'Good morning, sleepyhead,' he said.

She pushed his fringe back and kissed him.

'You once told me all the nights we'd

spent together had been memorable, because they were cold and uncomfortable — and then, of course, there was the lizard! I hope last night was memorable for a very different reason,' she said smiling at him.

'Completely!' He kissed her neck and slowly moved down to her shoulder. 'Was it memorable for you?' he whispered in her ear.

'Hmm,' she pretended to consider his question. 'I'd say it was acceptable.'

He pulled away from her with a mock hurt expression but when he saw her smile, he remembered how he'd described their behaviour as unacceptable before.

'Wonderfully and deliciously acceptable!' she said, directing his lips back to her neck. 'In fact it was so much so, I want more.'

★ ★ ★

'What if they can't take them both?' Denise asked anxiously.

312

'If they send a Lysander for one of them, they'll be able to take both,' Alexandre replied.

'But suppose they don't send an aircraft?'

'Then we'll deal with it, chérie. Stop panicking or we'll miss the start of the personal messages.'

They gathered around the long kitchen table, staring at the wireless, willing the BBC's personal messages to start . . .

'Before we begin, please listen to some personal messages . . . ' the BBC presenter on the wireless said. 'Why don't you draw a picture of the tree? . . . The peacock feather is colourful . . . Adam and Eve are leaving the garden . . . '

Genevieve looked at Yves. *Adam and Eve are leaving the garden*. That was the coded message to say he would be leaving that night.

'The photograph is fading . . . There are three apples in the tree . . . The angel is in heaven . . . '

'That's it!' said Denise, 'Genevieve is going too! Grâce à Dieu,' she added, crossing herself.

Later, she took Genevieve to one side. 'Now, you must give our love to your parents and Jean-Paul. I know it won't be possible to send us photographs of your wedding but please keep some for us. The war can't last forever and then we can get together for a family reunion.'

'Wedding? No one mentioned a wedding!' Genevieve said.

'No one needs to mention such things, chérie. But I have eyes. It was obvious from the first time you brought that handsome young man here that he was the one for you. Although for a time, I wondered if my instincts were wrong . . . But today, I am sure. Do you think your organisation will allow you to send a message on the BBC to tell us you've married?'

'I don't know. I suppose I can ask. Assuming Yves asks me, that is.'

'Ma chérie, trust me, that man will

not let you out of his sight once he gets you home.'

'*If* we marry, I'll try to get a message sent.'

'If?' said Denise. 'It's a certainty, chérie!'

★ ★ ★

Genevieve squeezed the silver charm anxiously between the pads of her finger and thumb as they waited in a small copse at the end of the field for the low hum of the Lysander aircraft. Men were in position with torches, illuminating the landing ground and ready to send the signal to the pilot.

Yves had his arm around Genevieve's shoulders and she rested her head against it as she looked up into the night sky. How cruel it would be if the Lysander had been hit by flak on the way to France or if the Germans were now waiting in the darkness ready to seize them all as soon as it landed. Or perhaps it would arrive safely and then crash on their way home. Surely their luck couldn't have held out so far only to desert them now?

Yves stiffened and then she too heard the distant throbbing of the engine. The men in the field now held their torches aloft, willing the pilot to find them.

'This is it,' said Alexandre, holding Genevieve tightly and shaking Yves' hand. 'Au revoir, not adieu. When the war's over, we'll meet again.'

The correct signals were exchanged and the Lysander came in low, the wheels touched down and the pilot taxied to a halt near the wood.

Yves and Genevieve ran to the aircraft as two women emerged from the rear of the cockpit and climbed down the ladder.

The four agents shook hands briefly before Genevieve climbed up. As she got into the cabin, she realised Yves wasn't there and began to scramble out to look for him but to her relief, he was half way up the ladder and smiled at her stricken face.

'Did you think I'd deserted you a second time?' he asked as he climbed in next to her.

'It crossed my mind.' She put her hand on his, as if to reassure herself he would stay.

'I'll never leave you again,' he said.

'Are you sad to leave?' she asked.

'A little. I feel like I've left the job half-done.'

'Ready for take-off?' the pilot asked over the intercom, then with the nonchalance for which RAF airmen were well-known, he added, 'Jerry was rather active over the coast on my way in. I'll make a short detour and see if I can give 'em the slip. All that flak gives me a headache.'

They crossed the French coast, drawing only a small amount of anti-aircraft fire and later, as they approached England, the pilot announced, 'Nearly home. By the way, I've heard about your work in France. Jolly good show! Churchill said you should set Europe ablaze and all you SOE people are doing just that.'

'See,' said Genevieve, 'you haven't left the job half-done, Yves. You and I have been lighting small fires . . . and others will go out there and fan those flames until all of Europe is ablaze.'

'With any luck,' he said, touching her heart charm. 'And now we're nearly home, I realise I don't feel sad at all. I want to spend the rest of my life with you, my Angelique.'

'In England I'm Genevieve and you're Mark. Do you think we'll ever get used to calling each other by our real names?'

'To me, you'll always be my darling Angelique.'

'I love you, my darling Yves,' she said.

We do hope that you have enjoyed reading this large print book.

Did you know that all of our titles are available for purchase?

We publish a wide range of high quality large print books including:
Romances, Mysteries, Classics
General Fiction
Non Fiction and Westerns

Special interest titles available in large print are:
The Little Oxford Dictionary
Music Book, Song Book
Hymn Book, Service Book

Also available from us courtesy of Oxford University Press:
Young Readers' Dictionary
(large print edition)
Young Readers' Thesaurus
(large print edition)

For further information or a free brochure, please contact us at:
Ulverscroft Large Print Books Ltd.,
The Green, Bradgate Road, Anstey,
Leicester, LE7 7FU, England.
Tel: (00 44) **0116 236 4325**
Fax: (00 44) **0116 234 0205**

Other titles in the
Linford Romance Library:

KISS ME, KATE

Wendy Kremer

When Kate Parker begins work as the new secretary at a domestic head hunting company, the last thing she expects is to fall for her boss! Ryan Hayes, who runs the firm with his uncle, is deliciously appealing. But beautiful and elegant Louise seems to have a prior claim to him, and what man could resist her charms? Plus an old flame makes an appearance in Kate's life. Could she and Ryan have a future together — especially after Louise comes out with a shock announcement?

HER OWN ROBINSON CRUSOE

Susan Jones

Serena Winter normally reports on local events for a travel magazine. Now she's landed her dream job in the Caribbean. On the Atlantic crossing, she's seated next to a grumpy stranger: 'Broderick Loveday, doing nothing and going nowhere,' he tells her. Her job is to report back to 'The Explorer' magazine on drunken monkeys and anything interesting in the islands. The kindness of locals — and someone special — keeps her heart in the Caribbean. But what about when the time comes to leave?

HEART OF ICE

Dawn Knox

Germany, 1938. The escalation of anti-Jewish attacks prompts Kurt's mother to send him to England but when he's boarding the ship, he's mistakenly given a stranger's suitcase. Whilst attempting to return it to its owner, he meets Eleanor but his humble circumstances discourage him from meeting her again. Their paths cross later at RAF Holsmere where Kurt is a pilot and Eleanor a WAAF but is there too much death and destruction to consider taking a chance on love?